THIS AND THAT

Leigh Clarke

Trafford rev. 05/03/2011

 www.trafford.com

North America & international
toll-free: 1 888 232 4444 (USA & Canada)
phone: 250 383 6864 ♦ fax: 812 355 4082

Dedicated to Beau and Bandit,
who keep me sane.

Introduction

In the introduction to Herman Melville's book Moby Dick, it was written that Melville never thought of himself as a great writer. He said "A whaleship was my Yale College and my Harvard." He wrote his book full of wild and untamable characters, in frank contempt for the genteel life.

One of the sentences revered in literature is Melville's opening line in Moby Dick; *Call me Ishamael.* The last short story in this book, began with an assignment in a class I took at Writer's University, to change the point of view. And I wanted to start with a sentence consistent to Melville's; I used, *Call me Moby Dick.*

This is just an example of the many stories I've written here. Given a subject or idea you write from that and see where it takes you. In most part I don't consider these stories anything except something I enjoyed putting to paper. I consider myself less of a writer and more of a searcher of knowledge through word. My struggles and excitement in the past few years in writing short stories, and a recently published novel, *A Land Above*, has filled many an otherwise lackluster day.

Please enjoy and realize writing is a tough master.

A Bright Clear Day

Nancy sang along with the radio, changing lanes here and there as she worked her way in the morning traffic rush. Her heart felt light and everything seemed to be going her way lately. She loved her new loft apartment, friends, and although it had taken time, late hours and weekends, her career in real estate seemed to be paying off. Approaching her mid-rise office building and entering the parking lot, she pulled into the space marked with her name on a sign, followed by Realtor of the Month.

She entered through the west entrance and greeted the receptionist, "Hi Peg, any messages?" She looked in the message center as the receptionist checked the stack of pink messages on her desk.

"Oh, yes, this one," Peggy handed her, "just came in a minute or two ago. He says he wants to see your listing on Oak after lunch today. Sounded like a nice, friendly guy."

"Thanks, Peg." She took the messages and material from her box and entered the etched glass doors. She smiled and greeted several agents, rounded the corner to the right and entered her comfortable corner office with a window view to the southeast. She turned on the lamp next to the sofa, rearranged the two chairs facing her desk and sat and started reading her messages.

"Hello, is this Bob? I have your message wanting to see my listing on Oak, is that right? Great; can you come to my office around one and I can show you the stats on the house, get some personal information from you and then head on over to the house. Would that be okay with you?"

The voice indicated he was in his car and wondered if it would be possible to meet her at the property as he only had 30 minutes before a meeting downtown; if he liked the property as much as he thought he would, he could take more time later today or tomorrow. Nancy hesitated. "Bob, I usually insist on meeting my customers at the office but if that isn't possible today, would you be able to answer some questions for me?"

He seemed willing and with her usual professionalism, approached the subject of qualifying for this upscale home, discussed his job and where he was living, his family, debts and all in the form of a back and forth conversation needed to qualify a buyer to her satisfaction before meeting them cold. She made the appointment to meet him at one o'clock at the Oak house.

Nancy stepped from her Lexus and approached a very handsome man standing by his white Suburban, whose appearance reassured her – his well-tailored suit outlined a long, lean body and said 'expensive'; his dark eyes were warm and friendly and she couldn't help wondering why a man in his thirties would still be single. His hand was warm and responsive and he said, "Thanks so much for seeing me in short order. I really believe this is the house I'll buy – everything I see on the outside, its location and price seems ideal for me."

"Bob, I'm glad to meet you and show you around. I want you to love the inside too, and I'm sure you will. Let's go on in." Unlocking the door, she led the way into the foyer. "Isn't this a beautiful entry?" she asked. It suddenly seemed too silent with only a click of the lock and a guttural sound back of her. Alarmed she started to turn and a hand found her mouth and what seemed like a knee hit her back and she lost her balance. As she struggled to see who was twisting her off her feet, she saw the eyes of a monster. They were cold and reeking of hate. His harsh voice was uttering ugly, terrible words.

The man who had seemed so friendly, warm and trustworthy had changed. His face was twisted into a snarl; as he pushed and dragged her screaming into the living room, he said, "Shut up you bitch or I will use this knife to cut you up into pieces." He pushed her to the floor and with his foot on her chest he reached down and pulled off her shoes and then her panty hose. Every time she tried to free herself, he drew the long cold blade of the knife against her neck. He took the panty hose and pulling her arms back of her he wrapped them tightly around her wrists. Nancy's fear brought tears and pleading, which angered him causing him to apply more pain; suddenly it seemed she had slipped from her own body as if she couldn't face the reality of her situation.

Time did not track - had it been minutes or hours? Would the office realize they needed to check on her? She began to disassociate – to reach out to a better place. Lost in her sobs, she could see her two beautiful daughters she loved so much. She thought of how she had lost her husband and son to a drunken driver on Christmas Eve ten years before; how the pain of their loss made her want to die. Now she had so much to live for, she knew she would die. This madman would kill her when he was through with her. She knew too much.

She listened to silence and realized he was not hurting her anymore. Where was he, what would he do next? Returning from her mind's journey afar, the paralyzing fear gripped her again. When would it be over – when would he kill her?

She thought she heard the click of the lock again and the door shutting. And then she heard what sounded like a car engine. Could he be leaving her alive? Her heart kept pounding and hope surged through her; although she lie flat on her face with her hands tied securely behind her she wrestled her body to turn over and after several attempts she sat up.

After gaining a little strength and with pure will she got to her feet and stumbled toward the door. The side panes of the front door revealed his car was no longer in the driveway. She opened the door with her bound hands and with all her remaining strength she ran down the steps to the middle of the boulevard, with the lovely trees lining the street of lovely homes, she began to scream, "Help, help, please someone help me."

Note: Nancy soon helped the police with capture of the criminal who had attacked two other business ladies in the city prior to attacking her. With due diligence she began to put together information she obtained with the on-line phone interview, her remembrance of his license plate and especially knowledge about where he said he came from; as she knew the town well, having lived there during her youth. She kept pressure on the authorities, and they followed through, with her help, in locating his real identity and enough evidence to put him away for a life sentence. Nancy remains alert to his appeal (he lost) and to any pardons. She is also an active member of the National Crime Victims Law Institute.

BLIND SPOT

James woke up headache throbbing; damn, hope I had a good time. Without seeing Rose in bed and smelling coffee brewing in the kitchen, he thought, lead me to a cup of that. As he stumbled towards the bathroom, he noticed his crumpled white shirt and jeans scattered on the floor. I must have been loaded. Hope Rose isn't in a pique. He dashed his face with cold water and looked in the mirror. His wavy hair was tousled about and his eyes red rimmed. Damn you are a handsome creature; he thought laughing and enjoying his own wit.

Rose sat in the kitchen sipping orange juice and reading the local paper. She did not raise her head when James entered the kitchen. He leaned over and landed a noisy kiss on her neck and said, "Guess you are mad at me for coming home so late last night?" Rose gave him no recognition, so he continued, "Randy joined Bob and me and you know how difficult it is to get away from him. He just wouldn't quit trying to convince me to run for that open seat."

"Come on - can the excuses. I've heard every conceivable excuse. Don't waste my time."

"You are brutal. What do you think about me running for office?"

"I think you are being used for your name not your abilities."

"Wow, you are mad at me. What abilities don't I have?"

"Aside from being a drunk you mean?" With James's look of amazement, Rose knew she had gone too far. "I'm sorry for that, but you've been drinking more since I met you. First I thought it was just fun times for you, but now I'm afraid you use it to cover up from feelings of being the 'black sheep' of a famous family. It's obvious your brother gets all the attention and is thought to be next in line for achieving your family's heritage – and you being the first born."

"Rose you are off-base. I drink with my friends. I always have and always will. You used to drink along with me and have fun too. Why have you decided to be Miss Goodie Two Shoes now?"

"Whatever." Rose stood up; took her coffee and left the kitchen.

EXPECTATIONS

*I have never told anyone this before…*kept running through my mind as I stood quietly looking out the kitchen window. I saw the large white cat that lives with his masters in the pretty putty colored house on the corner across the street. A medium sized yellow dog was sniffing the ground and approaching the yard where the cat sat silently. As the dog got closer, the cat pounced. The frightened dog ran whence he came with the cat hot on his heels. This reversal of expectations startled me. The big cat not only chased the intruder out of his yard but continued to chase the cowed dog until it disappeared into the straggly trees and bushes in an empty lot down the road. I smiled as the cat strutted back home all full of himself.

Reversal of expectations; how certain we become of our expectancies, I thought. Life is no longer a crap-shoot with variety and excitement. Still in a contemplative mood I saw the mail lady making her delivery. I went out and gathered the mix of junk and bills. Opening with curiosity the one I couldn't identify, my eyes fell on the invitation to my 10th year college reunion. An immediate response of no way passed through my mind; along with the usual excuses: Yee gads a group of middle aged couples with 2.3 children and McMansions. And more silently the guilt over a recent divorce, no date and what would I wear.

As I entered my lonely bedroom, I pretended to look in the closet for work clothes for the next day, but glanced over at the pretty dresses. The little black dress is too sexy. Well, it wouldn't be too sexy if I had a date. Then I thought of a college suite-mate I visited with occasionally and gave her a quick call. "Lori, did you get the 10th year invitation?

"Yah" she murmured, obviously munching on something.

"Do you plan on going?"

"Just a minute Peg, let me grab my wine. OK, umm good Pinot Noir. Well, at first I thought I wanted to go, and then I remembered Leonard and his society bride would probably be there. Are you going?"

"I don't want to go alone; Jeremy will probably be there with a new hottie. I thought of you and realized going together would reinforce my resolve to get over the divorce. Two hot chicks in little black dresses ought to raise a few heads."

"Let's do it, Peg. I will pick you up in my new convertible and we will howl."

"Great, see you then."

I had finished law school after graduation and landed a position with a large firm downtown. Jeremy worked in the District Attorney's office. We had graduated from the same college, but had only met a couple times. We were married within the year. I felt proud to find someone so gorgeous and talented. Life never looked so good. And then as my Grandma always said, "When things look great be prepared for disappointment." What happened still eludes me; with all the delectation of the beginning we found only disappointment in the ending.

Lori and I walked into the ballroom of the St. Francis. I saw heads turn our way. Lori was very tall and thin; I somewhat shorter but had maintained a slim figure. Soon a group of guys approached us on their way to the bar. The tall one with half a head of hair leered at Lori saying, "Hey, where were you 10 years ago." I walked on while Lori stopped and began laughing and chatting with them. At the gold circle bar ahead I saw Jeremy.

He glanced my way and smiled; showing his straight white teeth against his tan skin. Oh my heart. It has been two years; don't be a sap. Chin up, confident smile. "Hi Jeremy, how's the party?"

"You haven't missed anything. Glad you came I really didn't expect you. Was that Lori I saw you come in with?"

"Yes. We met again last year. She works for a tech company in the city."

"Will you join me at my table? I came with a guy from work, but he has been stalking the single gals, he's actually in the gang surrounding Lori. I've been thinking about you lately, and wanted to talk with you. Do you think we can shout over the band?"

We talked, we met again for dates, we fell in love all over again and this time I felt I'd reached the maturity to be a good wife and a good lawyer.

Now six months later I stand before our kitchen window on a warm spring morning and smile at our neighbor's cat. Jeremy and I both love to read Emerson. With his words in mind, we vowed, for our second time around, "To expect the unexpected, to end each day and be done with it. Tomorrow is a new day. You shall begin it serenely and with too high a spirit to be encumbered with your old nonsense"

I have never told anyone this before… but I'm through with old nonsense.

INDECISION

I have a difficult time in making up my mind. The last time I went shopping for a blouse to wear with some slacks, I went to five stores, tried on about a dozen blouses and never could decide which one I liked best; if I liked any of them at all. Then yesterday I wanted to try a new shade of lipstick. I thought I would like something in a cool shade. I sampled a lot of them and asked the lady back of the counter what she thought would look good on me. She made a few suggestions; I tried them and couldn't make up my mind. I decided I could live without a new tube anyway.

In getting ready for work this morning I wished I'd bought the long sleeved silk shirt I tried on yesterday. The black skirt didn't look too good with the green shirt, so I took it off and wore my kaki colored one. I really liked high heels with that skirt, but wasn't sure if I should go with my black ones or the half- boot brown ones. Finally dressed in my kaki skirt, green shirt and half- boot brown heels, I quickly combed my hair, brushed on some make-up and wished I had picked up the nude colored lipstick I'd tried on yesterday. I finally chose a coral shade and looked myself over and decided I looked just fine without spending a dime.

...And Then Come Back

Chapter One

They heard the explosion. Zack quickly rose from his chair and walked to the front porch; he saw black smoke rising in the sky to the northwest. "I bet another car missed the curve, that'll be five in nine years. Benny you stay here with Rex and I'll go down and check things out."

"I want to go this time."

Zack looked at his thirteen year old son, a strong boy with a heavy mop of straw colored hair falling onto his brow. So like Sandy he thought.

"Okay son lets go." They put on their sheepskin coats and boots and Rex, excited by their actions, jumped about in anticipation. The snow lay deep across the landscape; coming earlier than usual, and making it difficult to follow Rex down the mountain trail without their snowshoes. At the first clearing they saw the car in flames below. "Damn," Zack murmured to himself, "That curve has taken more lives."

"Dad, look. There's a body." Benny pointed to what looked like a form lying in the snow about fifteen feet up the incline from the fiery wreck below. What looked like a red jacket or sweater outlined the upper body.

They hurried down the trail; the car smoldered in its finality, enough left to be identified as a navy blue Mercedes sports coupe. Zack carefully made his way up the opposite hillside, slipping on icy rocks and then finding firmer footing as he approached the small body lying in a snow bank against a large rock; a bruised and battered body motionless and dressed in torn jeans and a red sweater; long brown hair partially covered her pale face, a young lady, probably early twenties he thought. Kneeling, he gently lifted her hair off her face and felt her neck for a pulse. He yelled to Benny who had lingered below, "She's alive. Go back and get the sled and put in a couple blankets and a neck brace. Hurry, we need to get her to the cabin." He took off his long sheep-lined coat, covered her, tucking it under as best he could without moving her body too much.

Benny found the sled and attached the halter to Rex. The dog had pulled the sled many times; with deer carcasses, logs and firewood; the large German shepherd exhibited a large amount of grit and determination and yet his warm eyes offered friendship. He located the neck brace in the first-aid cabinet, tied a couple quilts into the sled, and headed back to the floor of the canyon.

Zack prepared the guest bedroom and after checking for broken bones, cleaning her wounds and putting cold compresses where needed, he soon had the young lady in a pair of Benny's flannel pajamas and under the covers. She did not respond in any way to his examination and treatment. He smiled to himself hoping this pretty young woman would not be disturbed to have a veterinarian working on her.

The generator furnished the power to keep the cabin warm and the lights burning; otherwise, the large stone fireplace's flickering amber light glowed off the log lined walls. The smell of chicken soup simmering on the stove permeated the air. Zack had gone to the cellar to gather fall vegetables and a jar of chicken he had canned, remembering his mother's edict that chicken soup cured about everything. He reflected how over the past nine years he and

Benny had become self-contained in their mountain location. They did not have television or computer, but they had food from the garden, eggs and meat from their chickens, milk, butter and cream from two milk cows and they were able to hunt for other meat.

The next morning, Zack checked on his patient, who slept quietly, and then took a hot shower. Looking in the mirror for his morning shave he saw reflected back at him a tanned face surrounded by a preponderance of brown hair, mixed with gray, at his temples and some deep wrinkles lining his green eyes. Sandy always admired what she called his "strong chin". Was it beginning to droop? He put on a big smile face and realized it pulled up the line. "Good God, I'm getting vain," he muttered and quickly finished shaving. In the kitchen he made coffee and called, "Pancakes will soon be ready." In response Rex wagged his long tail with several loud thuds on the pine floor.

They had finished breakfast and started to pick up the dishes when the woman stirred and cried out and just as suddenly became quiet again. Zack hoped that besides her badly bruised body, she didn't have internal injuries; he'd checked her pupils and they didn't indicate concussion, but as soon as he could plow out the snow to the main highway, he would get her to the doctor in town. Another blizzard had come roaring in overnight and heavy snow kept falling in the morning; probably a foot at least, thought Zack.

He went into the bedroom and looked down at the pretty woman lying so quietly. He again thought of Sandy. He remembered the argument that sent her running to their country place and the terrible accident. "You're always too busy for your family, Zack. Will we ever come first?" She had asked for him to take some time off so they could be together as a family. The time never seemed right for him to get away. Ever since he went out on his own, his veterinarian practice had dominated his life for what seemed every hour of every day of the week.

After Sandy's funeral he couldn't focus. He felt guilt and remorse, but mostly he missed her. The doctors didn't expect Benny to live, but if he did survive he would have lifelong major problems because of his brain injuries. From this time on it was Zack's insistence on saving Benny that made life possible for him. Within months he made arrangements for two other vets to buy his practice, moved full time to their country place in the mountains, planning on rebuilding Benny's capabilities. And now ten years later Benny had surpassed all their expectations and even excelled for his age.

After dinner they quickly washed and dried the dishes and retired to the welcoming sitting area in front of the fireplace where Zack liked to read and Benny, when he wasn't studying in the loft, liked to be with Rex. Tonight he sat cross legged on the cow-skin rug with Rex's head in his lap. "I've been wondering why we've become so isolated." Zack slowly lowered the book to look at his son. "I mean, well, I sure would like to go to school in town. I've never had a friend my own age."

Zack sat quietly for a minute as if slow to react to what he heard. "Benny... I've always thought of what would be best for you. I know you've caught up with your grade – actually surpassed it. He paused again rubbing his hands through his hair and stretching his long legs out in front of him.

"I'm not saying I'm unhappy with just you and Rex. I've a great life here, I'm glad we aren't living in the city and I understand how you've dedicated so much time to me since Mom died. I've been remembering things that happened before the crash and wonder if that is the reason we stay so isolated. Like maybe you feel guilty... or I mean...responsible...or somethin'."

"Benny, you were only three when your mother died, so I doubt you have memories as much as you're remembering things you've heard me talk about."

"No, I remember you and Mom arguing about your work; she put me in the car and then I remember the crash. I can see and hear it, the skid and screeching of brakes before we hit the guard rail and a moment when it seemed we floated in the air and then I don't remember any more. When we found the women yesterday it all came back; we wrecked on the curve below, didn't we?"

Zack looked at his freckled faced son, whose green eyes looked back at him intently. He talked about this terrible day in the voice of a thirteen year old but the demeanor of someone far wiser. "Yes, your Mom was killed when her car missed that same curve. You survived, badly hurt but thankfully, another car saw everything and called emergency services. They airlifted you and Mom to the city. I think you know the rest and how we came here so I could be with you while you recovered. Riding the horse helped you walk again and Rex gave you spirit to work through the pain….. And, yes, I feel to blame for making your Mom so unhappy she ran from me and had the accident. I just have to live with that. But I don't what my guilt to hurt you. When you're ready, Benny, I'll let go, I promise."

"I know you will" He stood and leaning over he rested his head on his dad's shoulder and Zack stroked his hair. "Would you like some cookies and milk, Dad?

"Hey, that sounds great," he got up and together they strolled into the open kitchen.

Munching on a cookie, Benny looked towards the guest room and in a whisper, said, "Sometimes I think she hears us talking. Do you think she could?"

"No, I think I would know if she awakes enough to listen to us unless she is a good actor," he said lightly, but his frown lines deceived him, as Benny's remarks about their isolation created feelings of vulnerability for the first time. He would make changes soon, he thought, the outside world could not be kept in abeyance forever; he would do it for Benny, if not for himself. He got up walked through the hall to the guest room. She remained quiet; a small figure under the covers – her angelic face revealing nothing.

She was listening. At first she thought she had awakened from a dream; then a memory of driving rapidly towards the mountains and losing control on a curve. Now she knew this log-lined house had two occupants and a dog. The first time she remembered the man coming to her bedside, the light of day shown through the curtained window. Keeping her eyes closed, as he touched her head gently, she remained quiet. Had he found her after the wreck and brought her here? Was she safe – how long had she been asleep? All these thoughts were running through her mind. Alone again, she slowly began moving her toes, her legs and upward to her hands, arms, shoulders and neck. The pain she could tolerate; everything worked.

After the man left, she realized her hunger. Oh, how I wanted to respond to the call for breakfast. But I must wait and be careful. I hope my car is somehow hidden from sight, darn, if I had made it across the mountain I could have hidden it and gone on by bus. Her thoughts were quiet for a minute and then continued. I had to do it….

She thought about the past year in residence at the private mental institution. After graduating high school she had experienced a break-down. Under observation the doctors told her parents she needed treatment for her anger and resentment. Her parents quickly committed her to Tangle Briar. She knew she had been disposed of as rapidly as yesterday's newspaper as nothing must tarnish their position of importance in society.

With treatment Ashley became aware of the sexual abuse she suffered from her father; and that her mother had known but did nothing. Over the years she blamed herself and felt dirty and naughty and quietly nursed guilt into anger until every minute of every day was filled with resentment. When she was small her nanny tried to protect her and being unable to, would hold her close when she cried at night. Her father quit her when she turned thirteen and from then on he never touched her again in any way; his avoidance hurt as much as his abuse.

By the time of private boarding school the damage had been done psychologically; she excelled in her studies and musical abilities, but developed a cold core. It seemed every time she reached out for help, she felt rejected or others thought her selfish because of her privileged life. Outsiders only knew her parents to have the finest unselfish qualities.

Knowing her parents could keep her confined indefinitely, she decided to escape; after careful planning, one dark night she left her room, making her way down corridors until coming to the stairwell leading to the first floor, where several times she stopped to make sure a nurse wouldn't cross her path; opening the back door with a key she had stolen earlier, she quickly stepped out of the institution of cold walls and deadened souls.

Ashley stayed on the stone walk leading around the building towards the front gate and when about half way, tip-toed off the path, crossed to the stone wall and followed it until she came to the space between the wall and the beginning of the high wire fence, which followed the tree line around the back of the property. As she slid her body through the space, the guard at the gate turned his flashlight in her direction. "Who's there?" he called out. She pressed her small body up against the stone post and stood still until he went back to his station. Turning towards the trees she walked deeper in the woods and followed the pine needle path; the full moon reflecting on snow helped guide her way.

When she reached the street, she walked for several blocks to put distance between her and the institution before boarding a bus, using the few coins she kept hidden in a small purse. After changing buses four times, she arrived in walking distance of her neighborhood. The mansions on this boulevard all sat behind tall walls. She knew she would have to be careful to avoid alerting guard dogs that roamed the estate grounds. Since she had grown up on the ten acres surrounding the large stately house she called home, she knew the gardens, woods and paths by heart; an only child, she played and romped here for hours. She had a pony, a dog and parents not at all interested in her wellbeing. Her freedom became her friend.

And finally she was at the back door leading to the maid quarters. She knew the staff had Wednesday night until Friday morning off. On Monday she called her mother to see if she could visit on Wednesday, and was told "Daddy has to be to bed early because of a board meeting Thursday. Maybe next week will be better, dear." It was now the time to follow through with her plan.

Ashley entered through the maid's quarters and quickly turned off the alarm system. The moonlight through the window helped illuminate the large room. She closed her eyes and remembered how her nanny and the others always treated her warmly. She liked being here again. But I must hurry, she thought. As a good soldier on a mission she entered the main house and went directly to her father's study where she found the heavy revolver in the left desk drawer. With gun in hand she walked softly up the winding stairway to the landing above and down the hall to the master bedroom; finding the door ajar she entered as her eyes adjusted to the mid-darkness, she raised the gun and pointed it towards the figure of her father and suddenly; a loud sharp sound broke the silence; the gun rocked her back on her heals and she stood as if paralyzed, seeing both parents sit up in the bed, her father's cold eyes staring at her. "Ashley, for God's sake, what are you doing?"

She dropped the gun and ran. She ran as if he would catch her and take her to that awful attic room on the third floor. In the garage she found her Mother's car, fished the keys out of their hiding place, backed out and roared around the circular drive, punched the button on her visor, raising the guard gate, floored the gas pedal and soon merged in with night traffic on the main road to the mountains.

Had she hit him? Was he hurt? Would he live? He knew who shot him. Oh God, why did I do it; what will happen now? Her mother would be on the phone to the police, or, she hoped, their craving for privacy might prevent that. She directed the car towards the mountain road; they knew her fear of that curving, dangerous road that curled around hills like a menacing snake, and felt they would not look for her in that direction.

And before she could remember losing control of the car, she drifted off to sleep.

Chapter Two

Zack heated up the chicken soup he made the day before and he and Benny busily soaked their thick bread slices in it. Suddenly the young lady stood in the hallway door. Zack dropped his slice of bread and quickly pushed back his chair and all six foot two of him stood as if facing a ghost.

"A delicious aroma reached me and I'm very hungry." Her voice seemed older than her appearance standing there so tiny in the big flannel pajamas.

"I can't believe you're up and around. How do you feel – do you have much pain? Zack seemed to rattle off questions, not waiting for an answer.

She formed a small smile. "I'm stiff and sore, but don't seem to have any broken pieces, but could you point me to your bathroom please?"

When she came back, Zack pulled out a chair for her and filled a large bowl full of soup and put out more bread. He found a piece of left-over peach cobbler and filled a large glass of milk. He introduced himself and Benny. "Hi all, and who is the guy staring at me with the long ears?"

Benny responded, his curious eyes never leaving her face, "Oh that's Rex. Say hello boy."

Rex barked and wagged his tail.

She leaned to pet the friendly dog, and said, "My name is Ashley." She sat in the pulled out chair and quickly started eating, not raising her head from her plate until she finished. "Thanks so much – I loved every bite." She went with them to sit in front of the fireplace in the chair left empty since Sandy's death. Benny and Rex sat on the rug. Ashley sat with her legs pulled up under her; Zack couldn't believe her flexibility with only a day passing since he had brought her to the cabin. "I need some help in remembering what happened to me – I heard some of your conversation but it's unclear to me how long I've been here."

Zack, still amazed at her recovery, said, "It was only yesterday we heard a loud explosion and found you in a snow bank on the side of a ravine and your car on fire in the canyon. You had not been able to make a dangerous curve and thank goodness landed safely away from the tumbling car. We brought you here, treated you as much as possible and I'm so glad you seem not to be injured except for bumps and bruises."

"Did you find my cell phone, purse, anything?"

"Everything in the car burned. We aren't able to get to town for a while due to the blizzard that has buried us in for a few days at least. You can use our phone; will someone be looking for you?"

"No one knows I left town yesterday so no one is worrying about me. Do you get a paper? Have you heard any news on the television?"

"We don't get a paper or have a television. I'm sorry – we've been kind of isolated here and I just heard how much from Benny this morning." He smiled and glanced at his son. I've been so busy trying to make things better; I guess I forgot that he needs some outside stimulus."

Zack explained the details of their lifestyle and thought perhaps she would then feel free to speak about herself. She listened quietly and at times looked over at Benny on the rug nestled with Rex. Sadness enveloped her to realize how strong this family bond seemed to be. What could she tell them about herself? Would it be the lies she had learned to craft so well. Somehow she couldn't lie to them. Not now. "I'm sorry, I'm getting very weary and I think my legs are going to sleep. Could you help me back to bed?"

For the next two days Ashley woke up early, and with warm clothes provided by Benny, she joined in the chores. Since she had grown up with animals, she felt at ease with the menagerie of horses, cows and calves. The chickens puzzled her with their incessant clucking at her side, but she learned quickly to gather the eggs. Benny helped her feed hay and grain while Zack milked and then she learned about the machine that separated the milk and cream. They were hungry when they arrived back to the cabin where Zack put on the coffee pot and Benny stirred the pancake batter getting it ready for the griddle. Zack had Ashley tend the thick peppered bacon in the cold iron skillet as he chopped up some left-over baked potatoes for hash browns. Ashley toasted the thick slices of home baked bread, smothered with freshly churned butter, while Zack prepared the scrambled eggs. Ashley felt for the first time to be a needed member of a family.

Ashley grew comfortable with her surroundings and the friendly, warm man, son and dog as companions. They had not asked her any more questions, but she knew she needed to talk with them about herself. How much could she tell? Would they hate her and see her as the spoiled daughter of distinguished parents? Was she now a killer; a hunted murderer? The psychiatrist assigned her case had told her she suffered from the lack of self-worth, but did not have a personality disorder or any major psychological problem. In fact, she wondered why she had been hospitalized at all. But now, Ashley thought, her attempt to shot her father would only confirm their opinion for her confinement.

They sat around the fireplace after dinner; Zack reading, Benny and Rex on the sofa and Ashley attempting to concentrate on a magazine, with her mind elsewhere. "I'm gonna do some reading in bed, if I can stay awake." Benny said as he stood and crossed to the ladder leading to his loft. Ashley laughed at the large dog climbing behind; she had never seen a dog climb a ladder before.

"Good night, son. Sleep tight."

"Night Benny. That dog sure loves you." Ashley said, and again felt the warmth of love in this home.

Ashley and Zack sat quietly reading for a few minutes. "Zack, I'm sorry to interrupt your reading, but I wanted to tell you something about me."

Zack instantly put the book aside and a welcoming smile stretched across his weathered face. "You have my attention Ashley."

She began hesitantly and Zack could see a frightened child inside the confident young lady. "I'm not what I seem to be," she began.

She told her story and to her surprise cried uncontrollably when she came to the shooting of her father.

Chapter Three

On the first day the road to the highway melted enough for the jeep to plow through, Zack drove into town leaving Benny and Ashley to do the chores. He went directly to the library and researched the recent news - finding no headlines regarding a shooting in Cherry Ridge or any mention of her family name other than society news. There was no evidence of anyone searching for an escapee from a mental institution or a shooting reported to the police. He made two more stops, and then picked up some groceries and bags of grain, before heading home.

Zack jumped from the jeep and walked into the house. "Hey, Benny, I need a hand at unloading the grain." With no response, he headed for the barn. Bennie and Ashley seemed to have disappeared. He found himself thinking the worse – did Ashley take Benny someplace by force? He then noticed Comet missing from his stall. He checked outside and noticed the sleigh gone too. Just then he heard sleigh bells and Comet came prancing around the side of the barn with Ashley and Benny laughing. Zack walked in front of Comet and took him by the halter. "What are you doing Benny? You know you are not supposed to take the horse out when I'm not around."

"I'm sorry. I just took Ashley around the main pasture in sight of the house. I didn't want to worry you."

"It's my fault Zack. I wanted to ride in the sleigh and I shouldn't have encouraged it without you at home." Ashley's face held remorse.

"Okay you guys, get Comet cooled down and then I need a hand hauling the grain." Zack walked back to the jeep. He wished he had not felt the distrusting feelings towards Ashley. She had been with them about a month and every day he felt more certain she had been truthful and he sensed the year she had been receiving psychological help had prepared her in learning to live with her hurtful past. She seemed to thrive with trust and affection. He did not see any evidence of a troubled mind; and her remorse over the gun ordeal convinced him she did not have evil intent. And still he had felt distrustful.

After dinner and dishes, Zack said, "I have some news for you both. Why don't we sit down and rest before homework and reading and I will tell you what I found out today."

They assumed their usual positions in the large sitting area with the fireplace in full flame, crackling and popping and permeating the room with the odor of old oak. "First, Benny, I went to the high school and talked to the superintendent. I told him where you were in your studies and he wants you to start your freshman year in January."

"He wants you to come in and take some placement tests. By what I told him he thinks you can start second semester algebra without a problem and maybe test out of it and start with calculus. Of course, your classes will depend on how you do on the tests, but I don't think you will be behind the other students; maybe even further along."

"Wow, Dad, thanks for going to the school and I can't believe I'll be going there in January." Bennie sat on the sofa hugging Rex across his lap.

"Now, for you Ashley." She looked at him quietly; her eyes quizzically searching his. "I went to the library and searched the papers for any details about your family, a shooting, anyone escaping from the clinic, a young lady missing, and so forth. I found nothing.

I had to believe your shot missed and they did not report the incident. Probably they wanted to avoid any bad publicity. But to make sure, I went by the sheriff's office. I told him about your wreck and some of your story – not about the shooting. He searched police records and your name did not appear. You are of majority and legally on your own. So, I think you are free to go on with your life Ashley."

Ashley sat as if mute. She pushed her hair back from her eyes, but remained slumped in her chair. When she looked up she had tears in her eyes. "I don't know what to say. I'm glad if I missed my father – I regretted it as soon as the gun exploded. It jerked up in my hands. I didn't even know I pulled the trigger. Oh…. I can't believe I did it. I want to think I'm not crazy….but the shooting was crazy. So how do I go on with my life? Where do I go? What do I do? It seems so hopeless, even if I'm not crazy."

"Ashley, you're not crazy. We can do crazy things without being certifiable. Believe me, I know. After Sandy's death I shut down. I gave up my profession, my friends…..all to heal my son. It sounds heroic perhaps…..it wasn't, it was selfish; my way of handling my guilt. The selfishness kept Benny from developing friends and a full life. However, I have forgiven myself and am ready to move on. You need to forgive yourself so you can too."

He stood up and walked over to the fireplace. Looking back towards her, and continued, "I went to the vet practice in town, and they have been actively searching for another vet. I've decided to break my isolation and go back to work. If you'd like you could be my assistant a few hours a week. What do you think Ashley?"

"I can't think of anything in the world I would rather do – it would be everything I ever hoped for. Maybe in time I will find peace of mind and a chance for a successful future. I've always loved animals; maybe my future career could be in in veterinary practice." She laughed, and continued, "I'm sure that's a big stretch."

"Not at all, let your passions lead your way. You could work part time to make enough money to attend the community college, and use their counseling services to help you continue healing your early wounds. I think you've come a long way in putting your past behind you – one doesn't ever forget, but forgiveness can build bridges to your own peace of mind.

"This might seem corny to you young ones, but a Robert Frost poem I've always liked, seems to fit this moment; *I'd like to get away from earth awhile and then come back to it and start over.*

This is the time of a new beginning for us; let's get it right this time.

Note: Poem mentioned above: *Birches*, by Robert Frost.

FAMILY TREE

The branch of the old oak caught my eye. It began up high, drooped down to the ground and spread some twenty feet perpendicular; touching down here and there across the landscape.

I thought about my family tree; those long branches draping down to the ground – the beginning? Perhaps the weight of what was to come? Or perhaps the weight of what had been.

Grandma's House

"I can hear lilacs laying claim to the soil…the soil laying claim to the lilacs."

The house sits empty now since Grandma died. I approach the lovely 1900's two story white frame four-square farmhouse. "I can hear stars being born/stars dying…." Walt Whitman's voice again.

I pass through the gate covered with wild yellow roses, and look over to the lilac bush outside the kitchen window; so familiar with each blossom laying claim to parts of me. Walking up the three wooden steps to the screened front porch, I open the door and my eyes rest on the now silent swing, I remember the squeak of the chain as it moved back and forth. Now facing the entry door with the etched glass window, my heart aches for the welcoming voice I could only hear in memory.

The lovely mahogany banister welcomes me as I enter the foyer; its farmhouse style, sturdy not ornate, the anchor that seems to hold everything together. I touch the mahogany wood lightly and close my eyes. I can hear the voice; you are back, says the voice. The parlor still has the camel-back sofa and overstuffed chair with the pie table between that once held the large basket of photographs. Here sixty years of family memories resided. Only the voices of their images remain, the basket is gone. The upright piano sits silently against its wall; I hear generations of fingers on those keys.

In the dining room the glow of light from the bank of bay windows, reflects back the blue hazy hills to the west. The lacy curtains filter the light and create light and dark snowflake patterns atop the dining table. The voices of happy diners echo here in reunion and celebration.

The kitchen is the heart of the home. The aroma, even in memory, calls the hungry for morning coffee, hash browns, bacon and eggs; along with home baked bread, and jelly from the many bushes found in nearby meadows, wild prunes and chokecherry. Grandma's presence remains strong and I see Grandpa at the head of the table smiling over his plate of food. In between bites he issues forth his many stories. In the voice of his children and grandchildren you hear he is the world's best story teller.

I enter the hallway where the kitchen leads to the foyer, and quietly ascend the stairs; my hand lightly gliding along the banister. Grandma's voice is coming from the bedroom to my left. A soft voice, determined to make a harsh life gentler with her presence. During visits in my early years, we stood before the framed photograph of her family – father, in long white beard, mother, two brothers and three sisters. Grandma looked pretty at nineteen, with a high-necked silk dress and a lovely broach on her left shoulder. In my ten year old voice I would ask her to name everyone and she would, as if for the first time. Only the outline of the picture remained on the wall.

Slowly I descend the stairway, cross back through the kitchen to the mud room and out the back door, down the steps to the wooden sidewalk. I stop momentarily, look over my left shoulder, and send a silent goodbye to the lilac bush and to this cherished home before passing through the rose covered gate and back to my car.

"The voice churns with the nebulae churning inside every voice. This voice carries everyone, even those who do not believe they are returning back to the source of every voice."

Note: The opening line and above from poem by John Bradley, expressing how he felt when he first heard the voice of Walt Whitman.

HIGH IN THE SIERRAS

I stopped by for a visit with a friend who lived in Los Angeles. We had dinner and she told me of her plans to attend a 'conference' regarding communications and wondered if I would join her. The conference would be at a resort in the Sierra's for two days and I thought it would be fun. I must say I wondered about what 'communications' would entail, but I'd known Mary Lou for several years and felt excited to join her.

We arrived at the resort on a bright and clear morning; with breathtaking scenery and a relaxed mood, I envisioned a fun weekend. Little did I know how the event would shatter my calm and bring out feelings I'd never experienced before. I had heard of seminars in the seventies where they attempted to achieve a sense of empowerment; I certainly didn't expect this from a "communication seminar".

For two days, with instructions not to visit with anyone about the program outside the room, we sat for eight hours with the leader (communicator) assaulting us, in my opinion. We could not leave to go to the bathroom, we only spoke when we were called on and then we were told what to speak about. And that is when my problem; the situation when I reacted in a way that was unlike me happened. I could not speak, I sat stunned to silence. Communicator lady acted as though I intentionally sat mute. The more she attempted to get me to answer her questions, the more my "panic attack" persisted, and no words could be formed. I hated that lady. I felt anger towards her, she had no empathy. The more I tried to speak and couldn't form any words, the more embarrassed and humiliated I felt; especially since my friend, Mary Lou, glibly chatted on and on.

That night, although she couldn't talk about the day's events, Mary Lou said I looked pale and perhaps a strong cocktail and dinner would help. I had three strong martinis. It didn't help. I tossed all night; dreading the next day.

Sunday felt the same as Saturday's session, a nightmare. The 'dictator' perhaps seemed somewhat less authoritative, but I felt the same anger towards her and sat mute. The day finally ended and I thanked Mary Lou for the experience and headed for my car. Thank God, I'd driven up in my own car. I didn't want to talk with Mary Lou for one minute about the weekend.

To this day I am not sure why I reacted as I did. I'm usually very open, willing to learn new things, and mostly agreeable. Perhaps these sessions opened up a past I tried to forget. Even as I write about it, I get that panic feeling in the pit of my stomach. Well whatever. I only know I don't want to repeat the experience.

HOMETOWN

We gathered on Saturday night to see the new release at the movie theatre in our small town. A mix of six to eight high school boys and girls, though not dating couples, met at the corner drug store for cherry or chocolate cokes and then arrived several minutes early for the movie. The ticket seller smiled as she gave out the tickets and said, "Enjoy the show." Since we had already had our drinks, and spent our allowance, we passed the popcorn stand and went directly to the velvet curtains leading to our seats.

The pretty usher with her flashlight led us down the sloping isle to the front row. The lights were lowered, large sets of velvet curtains opened before us. We chatted some during the advertising and previews causing some seated behind to hush us. Then the main feature credits flashed on the screen and in the next two hours we transformed into the character of our choosing.

IT COULD HAVE BEEN

I played piano with the Modern Jazz Quartet. John Lewis, the main piano man could not make the gig at the Black Hawk. My best friend had bragged about my 'cool jazz' touch on the keys and he told Milt Jackson's daughter (a friend of his) how I could fill the spot. Strange things happen and somehow they asked me to play that afternoon at rehearsal.

I had listened over and over to everything they had ever recorded and sometimes even played along with them. And now I would be right there playing for real with the Modern Jazz Quartet at the Black Hawk San Francisco; home of the likes of Miles Davis, John Coltrane and Ray Brown. What a break.

After the first four hour set I could have played on for another four. The bop and swing standards really grooved. There I sat with this group of musical geniuses wearing matching black jacket and pin stripped pants.

SUMMER WIND

Chapter One

Jennifer sat on deck sipping coffee in the pale lemon and golden hues of the rising sun; the marina quiet except for the jingling sound of sailboat masts and the boisterous greetings of gulls. She loved these peaceful mornings before the marina came to life. Jake slept late after a long day finalizing some chart work and Jennifer reflected on the past three months.

She married Jake after a short courtship; made shorter by their desire to buy, outfit and cruise a sailboat for an extended time. Jennifer attended a real estate training class offered by the manager of the company she worked for as an associate broker. Somehow during this time, Jake found out Jennifer's love of the sea and jokingly asked if she'd like to go cruising. She laughed and said when should she pack? He took it seriously and started a whirlwind courtship. Jake had hit her vulnerable spot, and his handsome good looks didn't hurt either.

He wined and dined her and she enjoyed the attention. She had been divorced for over five years. He talked of his twenty years in the Air Force, having retired a Major after or heart surgery preventing him from flying his beloved jets. He didn't seem too interested in her life, and pretty much indicated he didn't like to speak of his, and it seemed refreshing to Jennifer to concentrate on the present and let bygones be bygones; after all the excitement of talking about sailing seemed to be enough.

Jake, however, had other plans for her. He quietly moved her towards the idea of marriage, after all, he said, an officer and a gentleman should be married when they made stops at Officer's Clubs along their sailing route. He made all the arrangements, bought the gold braided sailor's matching rings, and told her to keep things secret from the office. They wed on a foggy morning in late April in a pretty glass chapel in the Arkansas hills.

Jennifer went back to work and shocked everyone with her marriage news, and Jake had several more training sessions planned around the state, before they could begin the adventure. Her friend, Mary, thought she had made a very hasty decision that could be dangerous or at least difficult and didn't understand why Jake wanted to keep it a secret from her friends - unless he didn't want anyone to talk her out of it, or suggest using more common sense before marrying a stranger. But although she knew she had acted on a wing and a prayer, she hoped for the best.

In June they purchased Summer Wind, with money from Jennifer's investment account. She also put money in an account for maintenance and miscellaneous necessities. Jake had a pension, a small sailboat he sold, and otherwise no assets. They planned on living aboard until Summer Wind was retrofitted and ready for a planned cruise from the marina on Clear Lake to the Bahamas.

Now in early August they had refurbished the cabin; new upholstery, alcohol cooking stove, refrigerator and freezer, T.V., stereo – all the comforts of home. The books Jennifer had pored over indicated a true sailor would turn up his nose at such amenities. Topside and mechanically they prepared the boat for blue water sailing; new furled sails (a Genoa, and another small storm foresail), life boat canister, large bank of new batteries, a generator and a global positioning system. The dinghy, Catch the Wind, sat proudly upon davits astern.

And as she sipped her coffee and thought her thoughts, Jake came up on deck, "Good morning, are you ready to travel?"

Chapter Two

Within the hour, they cleared the jetties of the Watergate Marina on Clear Lake, Texas on a shake-down cruise to Galveston. If all went well they would be underway by the next morning. The day cruise went without a problem. They anchored, fixed cocktails and watched the sunset. After a light dinner they went to bed early.

On that special day, at first light, Summer Wind cleared the jetties at Galveston, entered the Gulf of Mexico, and soon her sails caught the wind on a port beam reach. They stayed on this heading until about ten miles out, and then sailed on a close beam easterly, following the coastline, and avoiding a multitude of offshore oil platforms. The day proved perfect for a good sail and they enjoyed watching the aquatics of the playful dolphins. Some swam in the bow wave on each side of the boat, as if to say, "Follow me." When Summer Wind became parallel with Cameron, Louisiana, they tacked towards shore to dock for the night.

The sun began its decline in the western sky faster than they had anticipated. Darkness rapidly approached. Sailors are warned not to attempt entering a port at night. They hoped the light would stay with them. But no, the night enveloped them before they entered the channel. "Get the spot light," Jake said, "Stand on the bowsprit and try to keep me off the rocks." Jenny flashed the light against the rocky jetty on the starboard side and tried to see ahead, but the blackness seemed overwhelming.

"Is the light helping you see the jetty?"

"Yes, somewhat, but I'm not sure what to do when the jetty ends and the channel to the harbor opens up. Try flashing the light ahead a little and see where we need to go."

Jenny heard their trusty little engine slowing down while she looked ahead. "I think the channel veers off to the right, but I can't be sure. I can see what looks like boats docked in that direction. Looks like shrimp boats."

"Okay, put the light back on the jetty and I will creep along and try not to hit anything."

Suddenly she heard a chorus of boat horns and at the same time the boat captains illuminated the darkness with what seemed like twenty or more large flood lights. She heard a voice on their port side and she saw a bearded face waving at them. "Just follow me," he said, turning his flood light in front of them. Jake got in behind him and soon they arrived at the pier where they would tie off for the night. This being a working port they didn't have the luxury of dockside electricity, but it seemed the space of their dreams now they were safely docked. These old men of the sea had helped to bring them to safety. Jake and Jenny filled the night air yelling out their thank you. They heard the chorus of horns in response.

This ordeal led to the decision to take the Intercoastal Waterway to New Orleans. However, the tales they had heard of sailing the waterway were no less frightening; large barges pushed along by tug boats hauling supplies and equipment created many hazards and closer to New Orleans they would have locks to navigate.

As they left port the next morning, their rescuers had already departed. They stowed the sails and the little diesel motor began its trip along a rather narrow looking waterway. They would now attempt not to get mangled. By nightfall they found a spot off the side of the waterway to anchor and were able to laugh about the two times they became high centered on a sandy bank in their attempt to put as much space as possible between Summer Wind and the work traffic whose wakes would push her up against the sandy banks. Thankfully, other boats created currents which helped to rock Summer Wind off and onward.

Soon they entered the Louisiana swamps and bayous deep in Cajun country. In their chosen night time anchorages they heard and viewed this wild land; beady-eyed alligators lurked in the water amid multitudes of cormorants and cranes. The wood ducks floated beneath trees growing thick along the banks dripping with Spanish moss. The captain's lantern, hanging above the table, moved side by side with the gentle roll of the water as they enjoyed their dinner before going on deck for a night cap. Sleep came easy and deeply with Summer Wind swinging gently on anchor.

Jenny felt going through the locks a piece of cake and when they approached the great Mississippi River, filled with all sorts of water traffic, she looked on in amazement of their accomplishments so far. They crossed over the river and wound through a channel leading to Lake Pontchatrain. The safety of the marina, after many days on the water, felt relaxing and after meeting many friendly boaters, they spent two evenings partying in the French Quarter. The mariners on the lake made them feel at home with their friendly and sociable ways. They also had drinks on other boats and shared conversation and drink aboard Summer Wind. Jennifer absorbed all the wonderful (and sometimes scary) war stories about life on the water.

After leaving the lake, they arrived at the expansive, lovely blue waters of the Mississippi Sound. So far on the trip the waters had been somewhat a murky brown. Summer Wind, once again on sail, purred through the clear waters, where the dolphin played and the gulls sang. In Biloxi they stored up on some fruit and vegetables from a farmer's market, and enjoyed walking the streets of this historical gulf port.

Summer Wind continued to sail off-shore by day and they came into port to anchor at night. The lovely turquoise waters and white sands never ceased to amaze them as they passed by Pensacola, Destin and finally reached Carrabelle, where they would cross to Tarpon Springs on Florida's West Coast; arriving on Thanksgiving Day. From here they would sail down the coast to Marco Island where they would stay over Christmas, before the next overnight crossing to Key West.

On a star-filled night at anchor, Jennifer sat on the deck looking up at the stars and sipping a night cap before crawling into bed. They had decided on the forward berth next to the head, even though the small cabin on the starboard side offered more space. After several layers of foam the bed seemed quite comfortable. Being of a V-shape the bed was spacious except for ones feet. Jennifer liked touching, and had chronically cold feet, but Jake always turned away, not appreciating being her foot warmer.

Although Jennifer felt she and Jake worked well together on the boat, she felt nervous about their personal relationship. Jake fell into long silences; his livelier persona seemed completely gone. Jennifer learned he had been taking medicine for anxiety for many years. After he had tripped on the boat and fell overboard twice while securing the boat at dock, he decided the pills had to go. Jennifer warned he should probably go off gradually, but he gave her his 'stare' and did not respond. Jennifer worried perhaps his personality change could be due to not taking his medication.

"Jennifer, do you plan on getting some sleep?" she heard his strained voice coming from the cabin.

"Sorry. I'll be in shortly, just relaxing a little. Guess I'm showing some nervousness about our crossing. Would you like to share a brandy with me?" She heard no reply. She finished the brandy and thought it best to go in and get some sleep. Tomorrow they would make the over-night trip to the west coast of Florida.

At first light, with a golden pink sunrise, Summer Wind, puttering on her little diesel, wound through the channel markers leading out to the gulf waters. They soon put up the sails, catching the easterly wind. From here the auto-pilot would keep Summer Wind on course, crossing the open water, to the west coast of Florida. They needed to be alert at all time for other boats. They broke the 24 hours into six 4-hour watches. Jake, took the wheel for the first four hours. As night time wrapped them in darkness, with only the light of nearly full moon gleaming down on the softly rising wavelets, Jennifer took her first night watch. She loved the freedom she felt there in the darkness lit by the moon. She would occasionally adjust the sails to keep on course and focused her eyes for any approaching boats or obstacles in the water. The wind in the sails and the gentle waves against the bow created a soft melodious sound. This is what she wanted to experience when Jake had proposed a trip by boat to the Bahamas. But had she been too hasty in her decision? She quickly brushed these thoughts away and settled into the night.

Jake and Jenny secured sails and washed down Summer Wind when they docked in the municipal marina of Tarpon Springs, Florida. They had arrived in the early morning and felt pleased the journey had been without incident and Jennifer thought it had sealed her love of sailing. "Really nice to stretch legs, eh? It's so strange how your sea legs stay with you for so long after getting off the boat."

"My sea legs are also aching," Jake responded. "Glad we can stay in port for a couple days for a change of scenery and some exercise." Jennifer noticed a smile on his lips and was glad he seemed more relaxed than usual.

"I've been reading about Tarpon Springs. Greek sponge-divers settled here many years ago, and it's quite a Greek community today. Supposedly, off the sponge-docks there are some popular Greek restaurants. I could use a change of taste and Greek sounds great - not that we haven't been dining gourmet aboard." Jennifer added with a laugh.

At that moment a couple, holding hands approached them on the pier. This friendly couple, who introduced themselves as Bill and Jane Taylor, owned the large sail boat docked at the end of the pier. They invited Jake and Jennifer to come aboard around five for cocktails and then, if they would like, could join them for Thanksgiving dinner at one of the Greek restaurants on the sponge-docks. Jenny thought maybe Tarpon Springs could revive her spirits and she would once again see the old Jake she thought she had married.

On board with Bill and Jane, Jake and Jane began chatting about real estate and Bill asked Jenny visited about the journey on to Key West. The Taylor's had been on the water for two years, their home port being New Orleans.

"How do you like your Island Packet, is it a 35? Bill asked Jenny.

"We love it, for a boat with a wide beam; it heads up well, and in a good wind we usually get about 51/2 knots."

"It'll be good in the Islands too with its shallow draft."

"You make a great martini, Bill. Thanks for having us aboard. We'd love to have Thanksgiving dinner with you. When do you want us to be ready?" As they parted with Bill and Jane, they gave hugs around and said they'd see them at seven.

They enjoyed the Greek restaurant, the company, and laughed about Greek food for Thanksgiving. "We might just make this a tradition," Jenny laughed. That evening she realized Jake felt more at ease with women than with men; somehow his gaze always diverted away from Bill, but steady with Jane. Complicated beings we humans, she thought.

The next two days they used dockside facilities for bathing and washing clothes. The marina had beautiful gardens and paths with many birds and lovely butterflies. Jenny visited the library, where boaters left and borrowed books from port to port. While Jake liked to watch the TV, Jennifer loved books. It didn't take her long to read through the popular fiction books she picked up.

They departed Tarpon Springs on the third day; Jennifer regretted leaving these friendly mariners and hoped to run into them again in ports afar. The course Jake charted would take them on down the coast; staying off-shore but again coming into the waterway to anchor at night. The easterly winds filled the sails and they seemed to glide over the turquoise water. When they finally arrived at Marco Island for Christmas, they had passed by lovely views of white sandy beaches and the cities of St. Petersburg and Tampa, Sarasota, Charlotte Harbor, Fort Myers and Naples. They would rest here for a couple days before attempting the next overnight crossing to the light entering the Key West channel.

******

"Damn it, Jake, I need help up here." Jennifer leaned as far from the wheel as she dared to peer below in the cabin. Jake sitting at the chart table did not look up. About an hour earlier he had reduced the size of the mainsail to slow Summer Wind's progress. He seemed worried they would reach the Key West channel entry before daylight. When the wind increased around midnight the reefed sails caused the boat to yaw from side to side. With the port side against the waves, Jennifer worried the boat could be swamped. "Jake, we have to adjust the sails. I'm getting drenched up here." She yelled it loud to be heard over the howling wind and the crashing waves. She could see the large waves approach in the light of a full moon, and as they reached the boat swept across the deck and Jennifer had to cling hard to the wheel to prevent from being washed overboard. Very wet, fearful and tired, she kept struggling with the wheel. After what seemed a lifetime, Jake came on deck and fixed the sails. Summer Wind now keeled to starboard and sliced perfectly through the water. "Go below and dry off and get some rest. I'll take it from here." Jake said in a flat tone. Jennifer gave him a cold stare and retreated to the cabin.

Chapter Three

After spending two nights in an expensive Key West marina they eventually located an anchorage within the Naval Air Station on the edge of the city. Jennifer thought to herself, well finally he can be that married officer and gentlemen. She couldn't complain of the location – they anchored in a lovely blue harbor among at least ten other boats with very nice facilities on shore for showering and grooming, she couldn't wait to get out of that tiny little head they had been using almost five months.

Jake joined a group at the club house who played Scrabble every day, and Jennifer enjoyed the time alone for catching up with bills and paperwork; although she hated looking at the decreasing dollars. She had tried to talk with Jake about the budget numbers, but he seemed to grow silent and distracted when she brought it up. Boating had turned out to be more expensive than she had planned.

They played cards often with a Colonel and his wife; shifting between their boat and Summer Wind. They also caught a cab together on Sunday mornings and went to a Cuban café in Key West for espresso and Cuban baked sweet rolls. They also liked going in for drinks at some of Hemingway's hangouts.

One day they received a call from Jake's brother who wanted to visit for a week or so and bring his girlfriend. Jake seemed irritated about it, but could not say no. The couple arrived by taxi to the NAS gates and Jake went up to identify them and bring them to the boat. Jennifer decided to give Bob and Mary their V-berth close to the head. On the second day of their visit, Jake wanted to take them out on the boat for a day trip and Jennifer pleaded for a reprieve and Mary said, "Hey, get off for a change, I'll take care of these old salts."

Jennifer caught a cab and enjoyed a day in Key West. She stopped at a salon an got her hair styled, wandered around the streets, with its unique occupants, and then found a French looking café and bar with a pretty water view for lunch. She ordered a delicious seafood cocktail with her white wine and then a plate of grilled red snapper. It revived Jennifer's spirit to have time off the boat and time to herself.

On another occasion when Jake and Bob went to the club house to play Scrabble, Mary and Jennifer shared cocktails on the deck. Mary kept looking at the clubhouse and then back at Jennifer. She seemed to be nervous; standing, looking over to the clubhouse, sitting down. She finally asked Jennifer if she could make the next round. With the second daiquiri in hand she said, "Jennifer how much do you know about Jake's life? Has he talked about his parents and his marriages?"

"No, really he is pretty silent about personal things. He said his father left the family when he was very young and he liked the step-father who raised him. He talks often with his mother and seems to be quite attached to her. I know he was married twice and has two children that are not close to him because his first wife turned them against him."

Mary remained silent, sipping on her daiquiri. After a few moments she said, "Please don't take this wrong, but I like you and want you to be careful and watchful with Jake. I can see you fit Jake's profile; a beautiful lady with money." She hesitated, stood and looked over the rail, glancing at the clubhouse. Jennifer remained quiet. Returning to the deck chair she continued, "His history has not been very good. He left Betty and the children for a rich lady and when she got onto him he took her out in their sailboat and put a gun to her head. I don't know how she got away, but probably promised him some money when they divorced. The next rich lady he married soon learned he was after her money and initiated divorce proceedings. He sued her for his share of her assets. The judge said he'd never seen such a cad, and sent him packing without anything but the old car he came into the marriage with. He threatened this wife too, I understand, but I don't think with a gun. His own children hate him and his reputation in the Air Force for being a gold digger was well known."

"Good God, Mary, I'm speechless. I've had some doubts about Jake, but for the sake of the journey and safety in not creating waves, I've remained quiet. He reacts with anger or a silent distancing when I want to talk about personal things. His silence sometimes scares me."

"Well it should. He must have inherited bad blood from his father's side of the family. His father was a nasty drunk and abused his mother. His grandfather was indicted for murdering his grandmother."

"How in the world did he murder her?" Jennifer stood and this time she walked to the rail looking over at the clubhouse. "They lived in the country and she always took the trash to a large pit to burn. One day when she lit the match and tossed it into the pit a large explosion killed her instantly. During the investigation they found sticks of dynamite had been put into the pit. The grandfather was indicted but they didn't have enough evidence to prove he did it. However, everyone knew he did,"

After Jake's brother and Mary left, Jennifer decided to remain silent for the time being and be careful.

Chapter Four

Spring came and they set sail from Key West to Key Largo where they would wait for an opening in the weather to cross the Gulf Stream heading for Cat Cay where they would enter the Bahamas. They met a fun couple who had sailed down the east coast from Canada. Their sailing stories on these northern waters where you needed radar and lots of courage, it seemed to Jenny, excited and yet helped her decide perhaps to stay in tropical water.

When it looked like time to cross the Gulf Stream, they left the marina and moored with several other boats planning a crossing, and at first light they set sail for Cat Cay where they would stop at customs before going on across the Great Bahamas Bank. Jennifer read the Bank is considered safe sailing with nine to 20 feet of water, but sailors should not cross at night or in poor visibility and they needed to read the water. Black, brown or white water is risky and blue (all shades) or green is good. Their destination was the Berry Islands and a small Cay named Chub, popular with sports fishermen because of large marlin in the deep waters close to shore. They anchored one night and then arrived at the pretty Cay late that afternoon. With Jennifer's new found worries about her safety with Jake, she felt safer in port than on anchor, even though this port was semi-private and expensive.

The beautiful marina had many large boats, power and sail and had expensive condos lined along one side of the shore as they entered the small harbor. The port master located them on a side dock directly below the clubhouse and restaurant and just back of a large cabin cruiser – probably at least 80 feet in length. After a nice dinner at the restaurant that evening, they strolled into the bar for a nightcap. The bartender said the large boat in front of them belonged to a lady who kept it at Chub indefinitely and lived aboard much of the year.

Jennifer started taking long walks each morning; going through a conifer forest where pine needles covered the ground in a dense mat. It seemed somehow other-worldly. She approached a rocky ledge and sat down and watched the water crash against the rocks below. The mist felt cool against her face. Further on, where the rocks gradually ceased and the sand began, she came to a lovely semi-circled beach looking out to multiple blue tones of peaceful water. With the tide out, she found lovely sea shells. As she walked further, she could see the private homes nestled into the trees with gorgeous views of the sea.

Jake went with Jennifer once, but later he said he needed to stay and do some varnishing, or other work on Summer Wind. Once when she returned from a walk she saw him disembarking from the large cruiser in front of them. The first time she saw Jake get off the boat, he said he had been invited in for a drink and a 'look see'. Jennifer asked if he liked what he saw and he muttered, "Okay." It seemed after that Helen liked to entertain him while Jennifer took her morning walk. Jennifer had never been invited aboard, but she had passed her several times going to the clubhouse. Jennifer thought she looked in her late fifties and although not beautiful she looked nice, if not a little too made-up for Island life. But then she matched her very expensive yacht.

Jennifer did not want to spoil a second of this once in a lifetime cruise, so put off any personal conversation with Jake, fearing his reaction. She thought about the revolvers. Much to her chagrin Jake insisted on keeping two loaded guns in the V-berth cabin. She became more anxious about them after her visit with Mary.

As it happened, within ten days of their stay on Chub, Jake, coming from the clubhouse back to the boat said, "I just called home and Carol, my sister, has terminal cancer" He said he had decided to end the cruise and go home for a while. At the same time, Jennifer's lovely daughter, Amelia, would be having her baby soon, so Jenny agreed to halt the cruise and be with her daughter in Texas, he to Indiana. Jennifer thought time would tell what this all meant.

They left Chub one bright morning and sailed north around the island to catch a route back to Bimini from Stirrup Cay, on the northern tip of the Berry Islands. Two nights on anchor in lovely sandy coves found Jennifer sleeping in the starboard cabin aft; sleeplessly vigilant. She told Jake she didn't feel well. The magic was gone from the trip. No more lantern lit dinners, just eat something and retire. They crossed back over the Gulf Stream headed for Fort Lauderdale. Her luck held and they arrived without incident.

Jennifer thought they might as well experience the best for what looked to her to be the end, so they docked at Pier 66; a lovely and expensive boater's resort. She sat on deck the next morning reading the newspaper delivered on deck and sipped coffee. Jake wanted to stroll around and see the sights. Somewhere silently in her mind Jennifer wondered if Jake's sudden decision to return to Indiana somehow involved the lady in the big yacht on Chub.

*****

Jake agreed Florida would be a better market to sell boats and they would begin looking for a broker. Jennifer knew, when the time came to speak of divorce, and it would, he would want half of any assets acquired after they married; that would include the boat and income from her investments. But this fight would come later; now she prayed Summer Wind would be cherished by new owners. She would miss her and long remember the best of this year adventure.

THE TREADMILL

"I'm glad you could meet me for a drink," rising and greeting her friend with a hug. "The fresh lime margarita is to die for," lifting her frosty glass. They ordered two drinks.

Her friend sat quietly seemingly searching her face for clues. The waiter brought their drinks. "This is fabulous," the friend said as she sipped the greenish liquid through the salty rim. "And this courtyard is unbelievable," looking around at the shimmering pond with spotted fish, birds singing in their cages, pots and pots of tropical flowers.

"Yes, I needed this today." she mused, looking around at the scenery and taking another sip of her drink. "My company laid me off today." Silence followed; her friend seemed unable to respond. "I suppose I saw it coming – the new management was not compatible with us and they brought in their own CFO to replace me. Twenty years. Tammy was just two." She gestured to the waiter.

The friend reached over to touch her hand, still silent. "Oh, they gave me a year's severance and I can keep the Lexus for six months. Generous as it goes. It won't be easy replacing a six figure income now I'm 50. I'd like to go for something less demanding, but you get so locked in......" She hesitated as the waiter approached. She ordered two more drinks and the friend ordered chips and salsa.

"I've missed so much of the girl's life. We lived well materially, but…" Once again she hesitated, sipped her drink and continued. "Anyway, emotionally I think Bob, the girls and I all face our own demons from me being so involved in my career. I guess you can have it all and not have enough."

LOST WITHOUT

Charles always arose at first light. He could not remember when he had ever missed a sunrise. He hastily dressed, made a cup of coffee in his new coffee café machine and started up the path to the ridge to greet the sunrise. Here on the ridge, he could look over the fertile valley; the land he had known for fifty years. After his parents died he married a neighbor girl and they worked side by side to produce a livelihood and a beautiful daughter.

Below he saw the old red barn which housed the dairy equipment where the twenty Guernsey cows filed in twice a day to give up their milk. He remembered in days before the electric machines how Emily would follow him to the barn and with her little hands she would milk her favorite cow Sugar. He would watch her little soft brown curls as they lay against Sugar's flank. He saw the earnestness written on her tender face. Sugar and Emily had a special bond.

Charles sat on a big rock that many generations before had sat on to view this homestead. The new John Deere tractor replaced the old orange Case that had pulled the disk through the pastures readying them for planting. Emily loved the Case. He hated to trade it in, but with the high cost of tractors he couldn't afford to keep both of them. His eyes drifted to the old Ford pick-up and memories of Emily and her mom coming home with supplies, all excited by the shopping, and calling for him to help them unload.

Tears filled his eyes. With everything he loved spread before him; how could it be the most precious one would not be there anymore. He looked upward and with a smile and hoped Sugar and Emily could renew their special bond.

Midnight

I decided to go down Dobie connect with Davis, turn right at Main, follow it to the bottom of the hill; turning left at the red light onto River Road, where I would find the entrance to the bike trail. The trail led along the bend of the river for five miles and eventually circled back towards the village square. The run felt good and I sat down on a bench in front of the ice cream house. Sitting there sipping on a cold water, I thought about the dog I'd passed back on Dobie.

He sat, chained to a post, in the front yard of a small, shabby house located next door to mine. His ears perked up as I approached and as always he seemed to greet me with a grin. I couldn't help but smile back. He sat next to a barrel, all rusted and bent, and obviously his house; nearby sat a dented metal dish, rather low on murky water. I hoped he had a food dish too. I smiled at him and said, "Hello there boy," he wagged his tail and I thought he had a very handsome face with big brown, friendly eyes.

I had moved to this small hill country village two months earlier to spend more time painting. I bought an old field stone house on one acre and converted it into a nice home/gallery. I spent my early morning on the exercise trail and painted after lunch for about six hours. When I moved here I hoped I would not be 'lonely' for the friends and city life I left behind. Strangely, I felt more contented than usual.

The next day, the black dog, with the wavy coat, sat on his chain, as if waiting to greet me. This time he stood up, stretched his body over his strong legs and lifted his tail up over his straight back and then put his front paws high up on the fence. I walked towards him and he licked my outreached hand. After petting his head for a minute, I told him I had to get on with my run. As I left, he stood there, his tail wagging and his eyes following me.

After these encounters, my heart would beat a little faster when I saw the friendly black dog. I worried if he had fresh water or if he had dinner each evening. I'd never seen him off his chain to get any exercise; except to pace back and forth in the small barren space. One day I saw a hunched over old man come out of the small rickety house and pour water in the metal dish. I moved a little faster and reached the front of the house before he got back to his front porch.

"Hello," I said. The old man turned around showing a frail face with frizzled whiskers. "What is your dog's name?"

"Midnight."

"I go for a run each day and I wonder if Midnight could join me? I could use some company and I bet he'd like the exercise."

"You want a dog?"

"I really just thought he could exercise with me."

"You could have him."

"Well, let him come with me today and I'll see how we get along."

"Ok."

Midnight looked intently up at me as I spoke to his master. He nuzzled my hand letting me know he liked me. The old man unhooked his chain from the post and handed it to me. I folded it in half and said, "Come on Midnight, let's go for a run." He wagged the tail held high over his back, lifted his head to look in my eyes.

I will never forget that first time Midnight joined me for my morning run around the bike trail. As we jogged along the river his wavy black hair seemed to glisten in the morning sunlight; he trotted close by my left heal and you would have thought he had studied at the best obedience school. I could see his eyes glance over towards the bank of the river where several ducks strutted and quacked in the morning sun. I slowed and we walked towards the river bank and I sat down on a bench. I let him sniff around the river bank on the full chain; knowing the chain would soon be in the trash.

Midnight and I spent the next ten years together. He opened my heart to the wonder of unconditional love. I miss him every day.

MISSING PIECES

When you begin to look at your life, you find many missing pieces, like an old movie reel damaged by too many years of viewing; stopped and started, forward and backward. Some things become crystal clear, while others seem hazy and you wonder if they are memories or stories you heard, and then you begin to doubt what you thought crystal clear. Only one thing becomes clear; nothing is clear; only subjective pictures in your mind's eye.

Note: I didn't write this – not sure who did, but it has so much meaning for me, I feel it's my own.

MICHAEL

Michael had long suspected something in his childhood had resulted in his deep seated fear of strangers and strange places. He lived a life of courage and bravery and no one would believe this hidden side. On the battlefield his bravery became legendary. In the thick of battle he would carry the wounded to safety, return and fight even harder for his wounded buddies. No matter the risks he took, somehow he survived to fight again. Only at night did the bad dreams of terrifying strangers in scary places overcome his senses; awakening with breathlessness and fear, sweat covering the pillow, he would lie there not thinking about the horrifying visions of war, but trying to understand his nightmares.

From college to West Point, Michael achieved accolades; a great athlete, a skilled musician, playing a soulful sax in a jazz band, and always an outstanding student. The girls liked him and he them. He had a muscular and yet thin build, his light brown hair wavy, and his smile infectious. But most of all he remained unaffected and authentic. And yet he had this hidden side; he concealed from everyone.

He tried to remember when the fears began. Maybe even before conscious memory? Michael had talked to his parents about early experiences; never admitting his problem. His Mom said, "We traveled to live in Europe for a few years when you were only 18 months old. You were a good baby, seemed happy, inquisitive and never knew a stranger." Never knew a stranger….how could that be, he thought. He felt no nearer to a reason for his fear. With growing perplexity, he tested his courage in every way he could with hope to eventually rid himself of night horrors. He knew he could be strong; even facing death he would not shrink from duty.

He seemed to realize in not seeking help, his courage failed him. How could he admit to such a problem? One evening, after a date with Ellen, a friend since college, he woke up next to her in a cold sweat and shakes. In his embarrassment he confided his problem. Being a psychiatrist, Ellen suspected stress from his combat duties. She comforted him as much as she could until he went back to sleep. The next morning over breakfast she reminded him of his night sweats and he attempted to pass it off lightly. Ellen said, "Michael, I have several patients with post-traumatic stress from the war; please believe me you need some help."

Michael somehow found the courage to talk with Ellen about his problem; about how it had been with him for a long time, even before his time at war. Ellen said, "The nightmares most likely developed from early stressful activities, or even more likely brain chemistry. But as you continued to be in combat situations the stress became magnified, the nightmares became night terrors.

Michael listened carefully and looked at Ellen in a new way; this beautiful lady had grown into a strong woman who gave him strength. She continued, "Together we can beat these fears Michael. You just have to have the courage to face this battle like you have all others in your life. This one will be the biggest."

Michael accepted the challenge of revealing his darkest fears. In time he could dream peacefully, and hold his new bride and doctor in his strong arms. He had found the courage that healed.

REFLECTION

I met Carol in the early spring at an Italian restaurant in the Memorial area of Houston. Our mutual friend, Grace, had insisted we get acquainted as supposedly we had a lot in common; love of gardening, jazz music, painting, pets (dogs and birds), interior design and we both were real estate agents. And if that weren't enough we were married and now separated from wealthy oil men; and we each had three grown children - two boys and a girl.

The drive on Memorial is beautiful; especially in spring time when the Azaleas are in bloom. I parked, entered the lovely Italian café, and knew instantly the lady waiting for me. She could have been my sister, except for her stylish office dress and heals. I wore Austin casual - a full skirt, linen blouse and flats.

We ordered gin and tonics and started to get acquainted. We both had two boys and a girl, and not only had we husbands in the same business, we had lived in the same school district. Her daughter graduated high school with my daughter. The coincidences began to pile up. All three of her children had attended the University of Texas, and two of mine had.

Carol had light brown hair she wore in a short style, mine lighter but similar. She even wore my perfume. She and her family had lived abroad with her husband's oil business (Libya) and my husband and family had lived for a time in Tehran, Iran. We both had family homes on Clear Lake south of Houston.

After lunch we gave a quick hug with promises to get together again soon. Later I called our mutual friend Grace and said, "You didn't tell me we even looked alike. We ordered the same drink, ate the same salad and good lord we had so much in common, I thought I had met my twin."

It is 10 years later and Carol and I enjoy our friendship. Grace is pleased with getting us together and as a threesome we have many a great time together. We make an effort to stay close and plan time for at least one overnighter in a three months period.

I never had a sister. Carol is like a sister and sometimes a reflection.

RUDY

Rudy did not swim across the Rio Grande. He did not climb over a fence, get lost in the desert or die locked in a truck. At age 25, Rudy obtained illegal documentation to support his impoverished family. It was the first illegal thing he had ever done.

The construction company doing a remodel on my home included Burt, the project manager, Rudy and two other workers. At 42 years of age, Rudy's residential construction, kitchen cabinetry and furniture construction skills impressed Burt. After three years on the job, he could trust Rudy to get the job done on his own and Burt appreciated his loyalty and considered him a friend. Rudy and the two workers lived in a town about forty miles from where they worked each day. Without affordable housing closer, they rented a dilapidated house in a small neighboring town that welcomed Hispanic workers. They joined funds to buy an old car they needed to reach the job site each day. Because undocumented workers cannot apply for a driver's license, they lack knowledge of the law and highway safety, and could not purchase liability insurance. They endangered themselves and others every time they slid behind the wheel.

One day Burt drove to Rudy's small town to give Rudy and the rest of his crew a ride to work, as their old car refused to start. "I'll be back by noon to take you to Dairy Queen for lunch," Burt said as he dropped them off. By twelve-thirty he had not arrived, so I shared a simmering pot of tortilla soup I had on the stove. They ate the soup with a basket of warm tortillas at the patio table. After they finished Rudy returned the dishes to the kitchen, I asked,"Es authentico Mexicano Rudy?"

"Si Senora, es authentico and muy bueno," Rudy responded graciously.

I loved to practice my very limited Spanish with Rudy. However, I knew he would say he liked the soup even if it tasted like dishwater.

Rudy grew up in a small village southwest of Monterrey, Mexico. For generations his poverty-stricken family lived as farmers in this region. Although poor, Rudy's family passed on a proud heritage and an ethic for hard work. At age twenty he married Maria, who lived in the same village where Rudy received his high school education in a Catholic school. Because the farm could not afford to support all the Sanchez children and their spouses, Rudy and Maria moved to Saltillo, about an hour away, and started working in a tile factory for equivalent of U.S. $1.00 a day.

They lived in a small one room rented cinder-block house. Bulbs hanging from wires in the ceiling dimly lit the interior containing an old blue sofa bed and a table with two chairs located in the corner where they cooked meals on a hot plate squeezed in beside the ice box. The grey unpainted cement walls did not have any cabinets, so a tall wooden chest with open shelves stocked dishes and groceries. The old torn sofa became their bed at night; they washed up and brushed their teeth in a small chipped enamel pan located next to the bucket of water they drew from the open brick lined well with a pulley to lower and raise the bucket. Their bathroom was in an old wooden shack located on a rocky path through a weedy backyard about fifty steps from their back door.

Each day at work, Maria crouched on a wooden pallet under a bare light bulb and worked with heavy, very thick wet clay. When the pains in her arm grew unbearable she visited her doctor.

After examining her thoroughly he said, "Maria, you have tendonitis."

"What can I do for it?"

"I can give you medicine for your pain, but you need to use your whole arm and apply less pressure to your wrists when working the clay," her doctor said.

Years of dust residue on every surface of the long, old open-air wooden building swirled about Maria every time she moved. The humidity of drying stacks of tiles surrounding the working area caused dust to stick to Maria's sweaty hair and face. The room stayed cold in the winter and hot in the summer. At the end of a long day, Maria stood and stretched her aching body and started the two mile journey home.

Sometimes Rudy worked with the crew that carried the clay from the abundant clay banks surrounding Saltillo to the factory where it was fed into hoppers with blades to cut and knead the clay. He knew how to run the hoppers and load the molded and dried tiles into the kiln. But more often, because he was a strong young man, he worked in the crew that loaded the tiles for shipping. At night the pain from this back-breaking work kept Rudy and Maria awake, but they felt trapped. They needed every peso to pay bills and had to face work early the next day.

Rudy and Maria were joyous with Maria's eventual pregnancy, but each harbored unspoken doubts. They knew it would be difficult to meet the added expenses a baby would bring without Maria's wages. She worked up to the day of the baby's birth. Maria's mother and aunt assisted the delivery on an unusually cold October morning. Rudy kept the water bucket and the large pot on the heat plate filled with water. He lit a small heater to warm the room. After a long and painful labor, Maria's mother announced, "It's a boy." A very worried Rudy sitting silently in one of the chairs by the small table scurried to Maria and kissed her forehead and viewed his son, who greeted the family with a weak cry.

By the end of his first month Maria knew baby Juan was not thriving. With constant worry for his well-being Maria took him to her doctor. "I am sorry Maria, but your baby is suffering from underdeveloped lungs." The doctor said after his examination.

"Will he be alright?" asked Maria with a frightened look on her face.

The doctor's voice choked to almost a whisper. "Time will tell, but I am afraid the results will not be good."

With a look of desperation, Maria asked, "Why did this happen?"

"I am not really sure, but perhaps the respiratory problem is related to exposure to dust pollution at the factory. We will never know for sure," the doctor replied.

Maria was steadfast in her attention to her baby. She carefully dusted to rid the house of any factory pollution they may have brought home; she walked with him in the early morning sunshine, cooed, laughed and loved him with all her might. But for all the care she and Rudy gave him, baby Juan died when he was only six months old. Maria and Rudy grieved for the loss of their firstborn.

Maria did not return to work after the baby's death. Rudy wanted Maria to stay home from the dust for her next pregnancy. He hoped that another pregnancy would help Maria in her grief over losing Juan. Without help from his father, who provided them with fruit, vegetables and milk from the farm, they would have become totally impoverished.

Rudy worried about supporting his own little family and his father worried about the continual drought affecting the Monterrey valley where low rainfall resulted in parched, cracked soil. Seeds planted in the spring could not push their precious heads through the barren earth. For many years this valley, where Rudy's father had his small farm, had avoided the drought covering most of northern Mexico. They planted fields of corn in the early spring in soil nourished by winter rains and later reaped an abundant crop of golden kernels on emerald stocks.

Rudy recalled days when he watched his father standing in silence before the living room window searching the high blue skies for any sign of rain. Sometimes when rain did come it also brought large, icy hail stones that fell to earth from greenish black clouds. Afterwards his father walked slowly through the fields to see the corn stalks toppled and torn. Rudy's father dwindled to a shadow of his formerly robust self. In time low rainfall, along with lack of credit and savings, forced them to abandon their fields and search for salaried work.

In order to help his family Rudy decided to apply for a worker's visa for entry into the United States. He was fluent in English and had honed his skills in homebuilding. If he could get a job in the United States his wages of twenty-four dollars a month, would be closer to twenty-four dollars a day. Rudy waited two years and did not receive any word in regard to his visa application. Maria gave birth to a healthy baby boy and expected another baby by years end. The family farm struggled to exist; his mother remained on the farm and tended a small garden, raised chickens and the hay from the pasture fed their Criollo (common cattle of Mexico) bull and two milk cows. His father worked at the tile factory.

After waiting in vain and desperate, Rudy talked with a man who got him documents to work in the United States. This began Rudy's status as an 'illegal alien' and he became a stranger in a strange land; quiet and separated from society and family. Rudy promised Maria he would always be home for Christmas. He kept his promise. He traveled back and forth at the border crossing for seventeen years; always worried his illegal documentation would be discovered. On his last trip home for Christmas he decided it was far too dangerous to return. New laws allowed illegal immigrants to be jailed instead of returning them to their country of origin. Rumors abounded about guards brutalizing prisoners.

Rudy called his boss, Burt, and told him he could not put himself or his family in jeopardy by getting arrested. He said he would use the money they had saved to try again to make a living for his family in Mexico.

Burt stopped by to visit Rudy several months ago on a driving trip to Guadalajara with his family. The original family farm was now out of production due to the continuing drought. Rudy, Maria and two of their younger children live on the farm with his aging mother and father. Their three other children and Rudy's brothers and sisters work and live in Saltillo or Monterey. Rudy established a small carpentry company outside of Saltillo. He keeps busy and his earnings help maintain his extended family. Burt said, "I felt joy to see Rudy again and to meet Maria, whose beautiful spirit shined through her bright brown eyes." The house stood old and run down, but everyone wore clean and pressed clothes and a large pot of red geraniums hung on the porch, welcoming visitors. Maria showed them her thriving garden of fruits and vegetables; and small reddish chickens picked up bugs here and there.

SUN VALLEY

I wanted some excitement in my life; I needed a change, to get out of the rut, to go forward in my life. For some reason everything that came to mind I rejected. In the rejection I thought perhaps I should look again, doubting myself, but no, I had not found anything that seemed right, felt fitting or otherwise relevant to my mood.

The next day, as I was walked from the post office to my car, I passed a travel agency and there a brochure showing a mountain in snow, the very thing that subconsciously I had always wanted to do. Learn to ski. I even knew where I wanted to go because somewhere deep in my memory someone said: "Sun Valley is the perfect place to go skiing." I didn't really know anything other than that statement of yesteryear about Sun Valley. Oh, I'm sure I had heard about ice skating and a movie by that name sometime along the way; probably from all my reading of Hemingway

I had a few extra dollars to spend and I booked seven days at the Sun Valley Lodge. On the day of my departure I flew to Salt Lake City and took a small plane into the airport south of Ketchum, Idaho. The Lodge, and what is considered Sun Valley, is north of Ketchum a few miles. There is great difference between the two; Sun Valley all about affluence and Ketchum rustic and laid back.

I marveled at the Lodge as I entered the large open foyer with vistas to the ice rink and snow covered mountains; the opulent dining room upstairs for evenings and Sunday brunch, the more casual dining off from the registration desk. In the large main lobby a large stone fireplace reached the high ceiling surrounded by comfortable leather chairs and a grand piano. Off to the left you entered the bar, a comfortable place all cozy in red leather awaiting happy après ski crowds.

The reception desk greeted me like an old friend and when I got to my room I felt like royalty. I spent the next hour or so sipping on wine I had delivered and calling the ski school to get registered for classes that would start at eight o'clock the next morning. I brought ski outfits, but would rent boots and skies. I felt the excitement of it all, too excited to stay in my room any longer and by 5 o'clock I headed down for toddy time. I entered the lovely bar room with huge chandeliers, walls covered with photos of celebrities and jazzy music playing from somewhere, The room seemed full of chatting après skiers, and I saw a few singles at the bar, so I approached and sat on a bar stool. I ordered a cocktail and visited with the lady sitting next to me. She too was single and a beginning skier.

I met several interesting guys and gals that evening and all loved to talk about skiing. I heard so many tales about the mountain, the trails, the pitfalls and pratfalls; I felt eager and yes fearful. But something within me wanted to be a skier. I did not come to find the "Sun Valley Affair," to buy fancy clothes or sit around too long in the pubs. I came to ski. I would ski. I needed the challenge in my life. I had suffered the "aloneness" it would take to accomplish something new. Walking into this unknown world alone was the challenge I needed to face. I had spent most of my life with a man by my side; ordering for me, taking care of all the travel requirements. I could not just sit and miss him any longer. I would ski.

Three days on the bunny slope had given me courage. Tomorrow it would be the big mountain; Baldy. It hovered over the entire valley. Trails leading from the top curved and traversed into the design of the "Ski God" on the tee shirt I picked up in town. Could I ever make it down a mountain so tall? Tomorrow would be the test of my courage. I would meet my private instructor at nine o'clock at the base of Baldy. I ordered a bowl of oatmeal and coffee, grabbed my gear and caught the bus to Baldy.

Travis said the most difficult thing I would learn that day was getting in and off the lift. I managed it to my surprise without a tumble and soon we headed to the top. The day flew by and after lunch on benches of other friendly skiers Travis said, "Ok dear lets go win your wings, follow me." We put back on our skis and off he went and I close behind watching his ever turn and doing the same. We went non-stop from top to bottom without a spill, without a stop of any kind. I had done it. I wore the pin he gave me on my hat proudly. Two more days on the mountain and I had changed. I had overcome fear and been courageous.

GRANDPA'S BARN

Off to the left of where I parked my car, downhill about 100 yards, you will find a well warn path leading to a long rectangular red wood barn. Before you reach the barn you have to open a six foot long wooden gate with cross-bars. Hanging on nails next the gate are two milk pails. Before turning right to the barn you can walk forward twenty steps and look into the poultry house and its 30x30 foot fenced area for the chickens to scratch and find food. The coop itself has nesting boxes for the laying hens and rods for roosting. About 30 white leghorn chickens are at home here.

You enter the barn through a Dutch door; the top opening with cross hatched panels. The first room is full of tack for workhorses and saddle horses and two horse stalls. A side door leads into a room with stanchions for the milk cows. Stacked around the south side of the barn are large bales of hay. Next to the barn on the north side is a round metal granary; and surrounding all are corrals, pens and sheds for livestock.

In one corral two horses, one brown the other black, are drinking from a trough carved from a large log. Seven little brown and white calves munch hay in an adjoining pen, being weaned from their mother's milk. The milk cows graze in the east pasture waiting for their evening milking. This large pasture, with tall golden and pink grasses scattered with tumbleweeds, is where a large reservoir and dam nestle into a rocky hillside where the pine forest begins.

Returning to the main corral and through another six foot wood cross-bar gate and looking left is the maintenance garage full of farm equipment; tractors, mowers, ploughs and other tools of necessity.

This is a working ranch. A man and his new bride homesteaded on this land in the latter years of the 1800's. The beautiful prairie and hill country of northeastern Wyoming demanded pioneers with rugged determination.

TANTANKA YOTANKA

Tatanka Yotanka waited for first light. Sleep intermittent; dreams of hunting large buffalo, awakening and then more dreams. When the sun first peaked over the horizon, he arose and dressed quickly and waited to hear footsteps approach his wigwam. Today he would join the hunting party. When his father, Chief Jumping Bull, beckoned him, he quickly stepped outside and stood tall next to his father; as they left to join the hunting party, his mother, Her-Holy-Door, called for him to come near, "You my son will be a mighty chief of our nation someday. The Great Spirit will keep you safe. Today you will be a man."

Fifteen braves and his father mounted their spotted horses and within moments of sunrise, through the pine forests, down rocky deer trails and onto the large plains they road silently until they spotted a large herd of buffalo grazing on the tall grasses of the golden plains. Tatanka Yotanka held his breathe with wonder at seeing the large mammals. He knew what he must do. The hunters had planned their strategy. Tatanka Yotanka rode the left flank with Little Wolf and two other braves, his brother Hearing Thunder approached from the right and Chief Jumping Bull and more experienced hunters approached the herd down center.

The late fall hunt rendered five buffalo to help feed the tribe over the winter. It was the time of year when the tribe moved from the Great Plains to winter grounds deep within Spearfish Canyon in the Black Hills. Tatanka Yotanka loved their winter territory in the tall pines surrounded by rocky streams of rainbow trout. One day by his favorite stream he said to his little brother Kicking Bear, "Let me show you how to catch the rainbow colored fish with your hands." Reaching in the water with a quick motion he trapped a fish against a stone and brought its slippery body out of the water.

Tatanka Yotanka heard stories of times when Cheyenne roamed the Black Hills. The medicine man said, "Our years of war with the Cheyenne are over and the rich lands of the Black Hills along with the Great Plains become home for the Sioux Nation. The land provides for everything; the bison provide meat, skins for shelter and clothing, bones for utensils and the bow strings for the buffalo hunter. Wakan Tanka (Great Spirit) is good to the Lakota Sioux."

At the age of fourteen TatankaYotanka joined a war party against the Lakota's traditional enemy, the Crows. "My son", said Jumping Bull, "The Crow, our formidable enemy are mighty warriors. I love you and may Wakan Tanka protect you." The warrior that killed Chief Jumping Bull that day was in turn killed by his son, Tantanka Yotanka. The boy's formidable courage against his father's killers made him a man and a warrior. He was now Tatanka Yotanka the Warrior. From this day he showed great courage in fights with the Flatheads of Montana and other enemies. As he grew, the Lakota warriors became known as "the finest light cavalry in the world, and Tatanka Yotanka symbolized the valor and greatness of the plains.

The American's frontier was expanding with white traders, trappers and settlers coming in contact with the First Nations. They coveted these fertile lands of the Lakota Sioux, and increased contact with the outsiders led to conflict. Warfare between the Sioux and the whites became general. Tatanka Yotanka had his first fight with the United States Army at the Battle of Killdeer Mountain. Later the Fort Laramie Treaty guaranteed the Black Hills to the Lakota in perpetuity. A few years later gold was discovered and Federal officials opened the Black Hills for mining. The treaty with the Sioux Nation was ignored; the Lakota would not tolerate this affront. The army officer representing Washington said to Tatanka Yotanka, "You must lead your people onto a reservation."

"I decline the invitation," replied an angry Tatanka Yotanka who had become bitterly opposed to white encroachment.

In early summer of that year the lodges of the Lakota were located along the banks of Rosebud Creek in southeastern Montana. Tatanka Yotanka sat high above the encampment sending a sacred voice skyward. He offered to sacrifice his own blood for a vision to guide The People. The vision came; he saw many bluecoats attacking the encampment. Later dancing the sun dance to WakanTanka, again a great vision came to him. He saw the attacking bluecoats fall in defeat.

On the morning of June 17, a scout reported the presence of General Crook's troops up the Rosebud from the encampment. Over 1000 Lakota warriors rode to the attack. They eventually drove Crook's force away from the encampment. Tatanka Yotanka, was pleased with his warriors but knew this was not the great victory of his vision. It was June 25, 1876 when the great battle began.

Although George Armstrong Custer and Tatanka Yotanka, were similar; both were cavalry leaders of great personal bravery, they stood for very different things. Tatanka Yotanka stood for the inalienable right of the Lakota people to exist on the Great Plains as a sovereign and free nation; Custer defended the right of his people to invade and occupy the Lakota country. Although numerous treaties guaranteed these lands to the Lakota in perpetuity, wasichu (those that covet Indian lives) continued to build roads, forts and railroads into Lakota territory. War was inevitable.

General Custer divided his command into three elements; a mistake because of the large concentration of warriors. Just as the vision predicted, Custer charged the camp but was driven back to "Last Stand Hill." There the Lakota under the leadership of Crazy Horse annihilated Custer's contingent to the last man. After the great defeat of the 7th Calvary, U.S. Army relentlessly pursued and harassed the plains nations. Tatanka Yotanka led his followers to

Canada. He refused a pardon contingent on him returning to the reservation. Eight years later, when the large herds of buffalo were gone and there was no way to feed the People, he surrendered and was sent to the Standing Rock Reservation. During his life Tatanka Yotanka married five times and had nine children.

He toured with Buffalo Bill Cody's "Wild West Show" for a few months; receiving $50 a month and all the oyster stew he wanted (his favorite meal). Later he joined a spiritual movement begun among desert peoples of the southwest. This was the Ghost Dance. The concept was: "If all red men followed this path the whites would be covered up and the world would be as it used to be." The army, fearful and suspicious of ghost dancers, decided to arrest Tanka Yotanka. During the fight that followed the great man who had served his people for 59 years was killed.

Tanka Yotanka, (meaning Sitting Bull) lived to serve his people, the Lakota Nation, who hold his memory sacred.

Words of Sitting Bull:

"I hate all white people. You are thieves and liars.
You have taken away our land and made us outcasts."

Is it wrong for me to love my own?
Is it wicked for me because my skin is red?
Because I am a Sioux?
Because I was born where my father lived?
Because I would die for my people and my country?

SEA TALES

"Go forward and release the anchor while I back the boat into position," Bill yelled at Amy, as he waited to drop anchor.

"Ok, it's down and has grabbed something; pull back on it just a little and it should set."

As Bill and Amy finished lowering and securing the sails, the galley hand came up from below with a couple of gin martinis and appetizers. Maria had joined them at their last port; a single Mexican lady from Guadalajara, somewhere south of thirty with a pretty smile and capable hands. She had come with good references.

"Maria is so sweet and a wonderful cook," Amy said to Bill, as they sat munching on the food she had prepared. "I never see her eat a thing, but she is so plump."

"Leave it to you to notice an extra pound. I thought maybe you would fatten up a little on our cruise; stop some of your incessant exercising and relax more."

Pepe, their first mate, who had been with them for the first half of their two years at sea, had laughed at Amy's exercising on the front deck. All six foot six of Pepe, a Haitian, existed on a frame as strong as an ox; his wisdom of the sea exhaustive. In his quarters at night they could hear him softly humming lovely melodies.

"Bill, if you would not worry so much about my obsessive dieting and exercising you could perhaps look in the mirror and see some obsession in these matters would keep your stomach from hanging over your belt. Pepe might have laughed at me, but he knew what it meant to be in good shape for a long cruise. He stayed fit by hard work and exercise."

"I interviewed a possible new first mate at port yesterday." Bill said, changing the subject. "He is older, bald and has voluminous amounts of tattoos. At first I thought he looked a little rough, but after visiting with him and looking at his references, I think we would like him aboard."

"I wondered where you were in the afternoon. Why didn't you asked me to join you? After all in close quarters isn't it as necessary that I meet him as you? I certainly don't care how old he is, or necessarily how he looks, but I really care if he is qualified as first mate and is compatible with the rest of the crew."

Not to worry Amy, he is coming by the boat later today and you can give him the once over. His name is Sammie and I'd guess him to be about 50 years old with very thick grey sideburns, but no hair on the rest of his head. He wears an earring in his left ear; got when he crossed the equator 25 years ago. He has been at sea in one way or another most of his life. His father owned a fleet of shrimp boats in the Caribbean when he was young. I know you'll like him. He is lean and fit.

"Well that's a good beginning."

THE BEACH

It was a semi-circular beach with pinkish white sand, bared and knurly driftwood stacked here and there; soft waves of varying colors flowing to its shoreline bringing shells to dry into grains of sand. In the far distance a fisherman, in water to the top of his waders, stood like a statue waiting for something. On the other side of the circular beach a long legged white crane stood on one leg in a similar pose.

In the peaceful silence, except for the soft lapping sound of waves against shore, a small boy sat on a stack of driftwood wiping tears from his eyes. He had straw colored hair, wore shorts and a white t-shirt and looked about six years old. Eventually he moved towards the water and waded along the shoreline; stooping every once in a while to pick up a shell or pieces of brightly color beach glass. He kept moving in the direction of the fisherman, but had not seen him yet.

THE GOVERNOR

The new Governor arrived on the Island in the late afternoon, greeted with bells and whistles and driven to the Governor's House; a short, stocky man with a full head of white hair and an ego the size of Texas. He soon renamed his digs "The Palace", ordered Texas Longhorns, white tail deer and his own personal horse to be shipped to the Island. He also decided armadillos would be a good addition to help rid the Island of pesky critters. Which ones he wasn't certain.

In the meantime he acquainted himself with the locals; returning to the Island from another location in the archipelago, he greeted the men working the airport detail, "Hello, my Guamanian friends; I love you." They were Pilipino contract workers.

When the animals arrived from Texas, he put them on display in pens and fences in the central square; posting guards day and night. Soon a photo of the Governor appeared in the local paper atop his white stallion wearing his 'granddaddies' big silver spurs on his boots with the large T on each. Later his spurs disappeared from "The Mansion". He left nothing unturned to find the thief; no one was talking. Another traumatic day for 'The Gov' came when four of the armadillo went missing from their cages. The story goes the angry Governor ordered everyone on the island be interrogated. For a week thereafter the local café's, roadhouses and restaurants had armadillo stew on their menus.

After he got into a drunken bar fight in downtown Agana, the President called him back to Washington. The Island celebrated his departure.

THE INTERVIEW

Fidgeting about in his seat, Sherman anxiously awaited his interview. This would be his sixth interview since he began his job hunt. He hoped this one would be successful. Instead of being more confident from all his practice, he felt more stressful. He began to feel like a loser.

"Hello Sherman, I'm Leon Winters. Please come on in and have a seat."

They shook hands and Sherman entered the room and sat down at the big desk, while Mr. Winters shut the door.

Mr. Winters approached him with a smile, and said, "I think you have replaced me already Sherman. You're sitting in my chair."

With great embarrassment, Sherman stood and took the chair on the other side of the desk; now more flustered than ever.

As Leon Winters sat down, he said, "Tell me about you."

Sherman had rehearsed for this question and felt more confident. "I was born and raised in this area. My family was lower-class working people, but we all had a good work ethic. My brothers and sisters had a lot of problems with the law. But I was a straight shooter. I was the first in my family to get a college education. I quit school a few times to pursue other things, was into stock car racing, but finally got my degree. My grades were pretty average. I could have got better grades, but I had a lot of other activities. I have had eight jobs since

I graduated, and have learned a lot. I always left when I felt I was not being recognized for my contributions and one time I got into a fist-a-cuff with my manager. He was a real Nazi. My last job ended a month ago because I wanted to find something I liked better.

Mr. Wilson sat motionless for a moment, and then continued, "What do you know about our organization?"

"I know you guys pay real good and have great benefits. You are a big company in our area and even though you sometimes get bad press about your big shots being overpaid, I would just hope to make my way to the top to get that kind of dough. I want to work for you because I like people. I'm known as a good-ole-boy to my many buddies. I get along with everyone."

"Tell me about your last job, Sherman."

"Well, I didn't have a brawl with my manager as before, but I saw no reason for them to be so picky about times on my time card. I worked hard when I was there. I think they let me go because they wanted one of their relatives to have the job."

"Why aren't you earning more at your age?"

"Well, I don't know for sure. I have a good work ethic, and have lots of experience. I just have not been recognized for my good work."

"Thank you Sherman for coming in today. We will let you know our decision."

After Sherman departed, the interviewer leaned back in his chair, looked up at the ceiling, and wondered how this guy ever got so far in the process. *Someone is playing a big joke on me,* he thought.

Danger in the Valley

Chapter One

The hot shower created a misty atmosphere in the room and Kate thought, as hazy as my mind. The mirror began to clear and in reflection she saw a face radiantly pink from the steam, framed by wet, wavy auburn hair and unsmiling eyes, as green as Irish shamrocks, and as deeply melancholy. She attempted a smile, and for a fleeting moment saw a glimpse of the old Kate, so sure of herself, full of life, the one with the forever husband; and then, the dam finally burst, she cried.

Attempting to calm her sobs, she returned to the bedroom she and Alec had shared for the past five years and stood quietly before the window overlooking the misty blue mountains to the west. It seemed to her an eternity since that cold, snowy evening she returned home from the gallery opening featuring her photographs. Bailey met her as she opened the door, but instead of his usual exuberance, he sat panting, looking at her intensely while she put her coat in the closet. "What you saying, boy?" Kate said, patting the head of their lovely red Irish setters, before entering the study where the image of the large rock fireplace created a reflection in the antique mirror on the opposite wall. She could see the amber glow of flames casting their reddish brightness upon the overstuffed chair by the fireplace where Alec always sat. She saw the book he had been reading lying open on the lamp table. Glancing quickly around the room and finding it empty, Kate thought he must have retired early because of his headache.

Kate left the library and headed down the hallway, lined with the many portraits she had of their ancestors, family and friends, to the master bedroom; Bailey following closely had her side. "I'm home, Alec," she called, and with no reply became worried. Upon entering the room she could see his body spread across the bed. She rushed to him and clasped his hand. He stirred and his eyes found Kate's and with effort he attempted to speak. Kate leaned closer to the lips she loved and heard him murmur, "I've called for help already." She crawled onto the bed besides him, speaking soft, encouraging words. He remained quiet.

Within minutes, that seemed like hours, the reflection of light glared against the frosty windows; no longer the welcoming glow of the fireplace. The siren tore through the silence.

Kate rushed to the front door. The paramedics quickly put Alec on the gurney and into the ambulance. Bailey kept whining and Kate said, "It'll be okay boy." She didn't want to leave Alec's side, but knew she'd need her car, so she quickly put on her coat, told Baily she would be back soon, leaving him forlorn in the foyer. The chill of the mountain air increased the trembling born of anxiety and worry. The curvy snow covered road seemed to go on forever as she followed the tail lights ahead. Suddenly she remembered to call Dr. Wilson, so he would be at the hospital when Alec arrived.

Arriving at the emergency entrance; Kate parked in visitors parking while the paramedics got Alec into the emergency room. When she entered, nurses and interns surrounded Alec. Kate marveled at their efficiency, but Alec's pale and still countenance brought back the deep fear in her. "Will he be okay?" was all she could manage to say.

"We'll take good care of him," a voice behind her said. She looked back to see Dr. Wilson enter the room.

"Oh, thank God you're here Paul. Alec stayed home from the gallery opening this evening because of a bad headache. I found him on the bed when I got home. He could barely talk, or move. Do you think he's had a stroke?"

"We'll get him stabilized and admit him to intensive care. It'll be hours before we know anything."

Kate sat quietly in the corner of the intensive care waiting room filled with people that also seemed in shock, she thought. She got a strong coffee from the table offering drinks, sat back down hoping the warmth of the coffee would stop her shivering.

In the fear of her silence, memories flooded Kate's mind. She and Alec had both grown up in this small town located in the green valley surrounded by mountains. She remembered the stories of how their ancestor's arrived in dirty, dusty and worn covered wagons after months on dangerous trails, mountain crossings and river fording; many suffering from disease and leaving their dead along the way. The surviving families united to build log cabins with sod floors, planted crops and started cattle herds from the few they brought west with them. They worked together to build school houses and community churches and thanked God for their blessings.

Alec and Kate's parents belonged to this ancestry; The Bennett's owned a large ranch passed down for four generations, and Kate's dad owned the local feed company which had been owned by three generations of McLeans. She and Alec met for the first time when they started first grade; he, with the slanted grin and shock of dark hair on his forehead, she with long chestnut hair with a red glow and two missing front teeth. Alec came to her rescue at recess when a troubled classmate trapped her in a basement walkway and began choking her. She had been devoted to him ever since, she thought.

Kate realized her reminiscing had allowed three hours to pass. She finally dozed a little and soon it was morning. Kate found a nurse who said Alec had attendants with him, but she would let Kate know when she could see him. She sipped coffee and waited.

It seemed hours had passed before the nurse came back, and Kate leaped up and went to her side. "How is he? Can I see him?"

"Yes, Mrs. Bennett, you can see him for a minute but he is still unconscious, so be prepared." Kate followed her to Alec's beside. He lay there so still, with the tousled hair she loved resting on his forehead. The monitors and machines hooked up to his body beeped with rhythmic sounds. She took his hand and spoke to him gently. "I'm here, honey.

Later, with Alec still unconscious, Kate, emotionally exhausted, left the hospital and drove home. She arrived in front of the old rock house and could see the front door ajar. Knowing she had rushed out without setting the alarm, Kate also wondered if she had not been careful about locking up as well. Bailey greeted her as she stepped out of the car his large brown eyes seemed fearful and his anxious panting seemed to say something's wrong. Upon entering the foyer, she saw the living room sofas and chairs strewn about with their cushions on the floor and tables overturned. Had her world gone mad, she thought, and in panic she turned around, the feeling of being trapped rising in her throat; and ran back towards the car and called the police.

Chapter Two

The police detectives and investigators began gathering evidence. Detective Bell asked if she had any idea what the intruders were looking for and although Kate knew she should tell him about the disks Alec had put in the secret vault, she withheld this, knowing their importance to Alec and not wanting to ruin his investigation. When everyone left, she quickly found the vault had not been discovered by the intruders.

Kate fed Bailey, took a shower and put on clean clothes. She hated leaving Bailey again and she could tell he didn't want her to leave. She gave him a big hug and left him sitting patiently on the front porch. This big, loveable Irish setter, had a friendly nature, but Kate worried he might have been hurt by the intruders if he had been more aggressive.

When she arrived at the intensive care unit, Kate found Dr. Wilson just arriving. "Have you been able to determine what is going on yet?" she asked.

"It's strange. His tests aren't specific in regard to any one problem. It's definitely not his heart, or a stroke and it'll take some time to get the toxicology report back. You said he hasn't taken anything except aspirin and he's not on any prescription medicines, but there's an indication he's been poisoned."

"Oh, my God, Paul. I can't imagine that's true." She thought instantly of a photo shoot Alec asked her for and how he had warned her as to be careful he was in the midst of an investigation that might put us in some peril; and then his sudden sickness and the break-in overnight. She thought to herself, what are we dealing with here?

"Try not to worry too much Kate. We're taking good care of him. It'll help to know for sure what kind of poison it is, if it is poison.

We're taking preventative measures to keep him from becoming sicker, and we'll attempt to rush the reports."

Later that day they moved Alec and his machines into a private suite where Kate could talk and read to Alec without bothering anyone; she read from the mystery Alec had next to his chair in the study; starting at the beginning, she hoped optimistically Alec wouldn't mind hearing it a second time.

As evening approached, Kate said, "I'll leave you for now, sweetheart," "I need to tend to Bailey and maybe get a little rest." She kissed him softly on his quiet brow. She felt sleep deprived and would be glad to get home; although she knew she would be nervous after yesterday's break-in. Bailey greeted her with kisses upon her arrival home and his presence was reassuring. She carefully locked up and set the security alarm, other than that she was just too tired to get her mind around everything.

By the end of the first week, Alec stabilized but remained unconscious. His parents came to be with him and Kate spent as much time as she could, reading, talking, holding his hand and hoping for a response. She told him she had been going to the office every morning and Judy had everything under control. Judy told her the new reporter he had hired suddenly turned in his resignation and wanted to leave immediately.

One morning before she left for the hospital, Dr. Wilson called, "Kate, would you please come by my office this morning, I need to visit with you."

"Paul," she said in panic, "What is it?"

"Kate, the toxicology report is in. How soon can you be here?"

"I'll be leaving in the next half hour."

Kate felt anxious for she heard tension in Paul's voice. God, she though, this just can't be more bad news." Within the hour Kate sat across from the doctor. He said, "It was arsenic that made Alec sick, Kate, but thank God, it's not an acute poisoning, and we should be able to cure him completely. It's obvious the poison accumulated in his system and over time it caused his body to shut down."

Kate sat speechless. She couldn't believe what she heard. Who could have been poisoning Alec and how would they have done it?

It just didn't make sense. Dr. Wilson continued. "The police are involved now Kate. It'll be investigated as an attempted murder case. I wanted you to realize they'll be looking at you closely. You're the one closest to him and would have the most opportunity. I wanted you to know we had to notify them."

"It's okay, Paul; I've nothing to fear and they'll soon find I'm not the guilty one. It's time to find out who is, and I'll help them in every way I can. How long do you think it'll be before Alec will gain consciousness?"

"With the procedure we begin now, it shouldn't be long. He should be back to normal in a couple more weeks."

Kate thanked Dr. Wilson for the heads up and decided to visit with Alec after lunch and for now go back home and get her head cleared. She supposed the police would be contacting her soon. Before she even reached the circular drive, she had a call on her cell phone. She wanted to ignore it. Enough is enough, she thought. From the dial she could see it was the police department.

"Hello."

"Is this Mrs. Bennett?" the voice asked.

"Yes, this is Kate Bennett. May I help you?"

"We would like you to come to the precinct this afternoon, Mrs. Bennett. The Chief would like to see you."

"Right; what time should I be there?"

"Be here by two."

Things are happening too fast, she thought. She knew she could clear things up. She only wished Alec could approve what she knew she must do. But time could not wait and she would have to handle this herself.

Kate entered the Chief's office and he looked up with a smile and said, "Hi Kate, sorry we have to call you in when you have so much worry with Alec, but I must follow procedure."

Bryan Harris had known Alec since childhood. Kate and Alec had established a good friendship with Bryan and his wife Ann. Last winter they had gone on a sailing trip together in the Caribbean. She knew his interrogation would be thorough to avoid any sign of impropriety.

"I know Bryan, and I want to cooperate fully. I've brought some things that will help this case. I failed to be altogether forthcoming with your Detective Bell at the scene of the break-in as I hoped Alec would be able to tell me what to do, but now I know I must go ahead and help you get to the bottom of these terrible circumstances."

Kate pulled from her bag the ten computer disks Alec had burned and put in the hidden vault; she had spent hours the night before going through them discovering details that surprised her. Alec had been very thorough in his investigation.

"Alec has been working on an expose of contamination problems at the Hammond storage facility for the past year, Kate began. "I took photos of two corporate guys meeting with the site engineer, the new reporter Alec had hired, and a large rough looking character. Then, with a source's help, I got some shots of the storage facility with a telephoto lens. Before I could get them to Alec, he was sick in the hospital."

As Kate continued, Bryan sat quietly listening. "Alec first started investigating measures needed to improve security of facilities holding dangerous amounts of radiation materials. He found one company in particular cutting corners to save on costs. Unknown to any of us, Alec brought in experts to do an air-toxic study and a ground water contamination study; these studies showed low amounts of radiation, along with other dangerous chemicals, both in the air and in the watershed."

Kate stopped for a sip of water, and continued, "It's now obvious Alec knew Ron Adams, his new hire, was reporting everything he could find out about Alec's investigation to these corporate guys. That's why Alec was so careful to bring his work home and put the disks away in our hidden vault. Thank goodness they weren't found during the break-in. As I read all of this information last night, I remembered Alec complaining about the coffee at the office tasting bitter lately. He was the only coffee drinker and since the new reporter left town shortly after Alec became sick, I'd check the coffee at the office to see if it's the source of the poison."

As Kate sat back in her chair apparently out of words, Bryan quickly picked up the conversation, "This is all very important information, please leave the CD's and photographs with me. I'm sorry for the troubles you're having Kate. We'll keep an eye out to keep you safe until we get these criminals and put them behind bars where they belong." Bryan thanked her for coming by and added, "Please tell Alec that Ann and I are praying for his full recovery."

Chapter Three

On her drive home Kate remembered how soon after she and Alec moved back to the valley and Alec had settled into his position as owner and editorial writer for the Daily Record, they began to hear growing alarm from friends and neighbors of a scourge devastating their beloved valley. It seemed within a very short time the western slope had been dotted with derricks and black iron pumps. At first, large trucks carrying heavy loads of pipe and equipment tore up the land and knocked down fences; stacks of pipe, large pits for water and piles of sand needed to drill oil and gas wells lay scattered around the location and foul air created by all this activity remained trapped in the valley by the mountains causing health problems for the residents as well as consternation over the unsightliness brought to the valley.

Alec soon found the government had given out hundreds of permits for oil and gas drilling on all federal lands. He immediately set out to investigate what could be done. He published articles on solutions to ease the pollution; both in air and ground water and attempted to negotiate with the energy companies to clean-up their sites, all to no avail, while reports kept coming about residents complaining of headaches, skin irritation, nausea and dizziness. The company men simply stated their operations could not be faulted and no medical data could prove a link to health problems. Alec set up town hall meetings, to allow the executives, managers, and engineers, to talk with the valley's residents about their fears; they refused the invitation. The contacts he made with the state and federal government environmental offices brought no results as the large push in the country for more oil and gas had all but eliminated restrictions on energy company's activities.

Early one crisp winter morning, Alec seemed rushed; putting on his jacket as he entered the kitchen, he said, "Kate, I need to be at the office early this morning and since I'm running late, I'll just grab some breakfast later."

"No problem. I haven't fixed anything but coffee."

"Great, I'll take a cup with me. Judy has reverted to some bitter old-time reporter's mud; it's so bitter the new guy I hired won't touch it. By the way, will you be able to get the photos to me by tomorrow?"

"Sure, I've already taken most of them. The remaining will be just a little more difficult to shoot, but I've a source I'm meeting at four this afternoon; we should be in and out fast, and I'll develop them and bring all of them to you by tomorrow. What is the name of your new reporter?"

"Ron Adams. Rather a strange dude; seems to be always lurking in the shadows. You watch your back taking the photos. These guys can be tough." He leaned down and brushed her cheek with his lips and headed for the door. Her eyes followed his lean, sexy body, wishing he wasn't in such a hurry.

As Alec opened the front door, she exclaimed, "You be careful too. It's your investigation that'll set off fireworks."

He grinned back at her and was off.

She remembered how Alec brought home a brief case full of paper each evening to work on after dinner and long into the night. Kate saw him put disks in their secret vault before he shut down the computer and came to bed. Her curiosity peaked, but she knew he would share details when he had all the facts. Kate knew the investigation he'd been conducting involved the photos she gathered for him of oil company men and today she'd shoot film at the storage facility on a site near town. A source could get her close enough to use her telephoto lens.

Kate hurried home after the shoot to prepare dinner before the gallery opening that evening. The lemon chicken with pesto sauce and pasta was ready when she heard Alec come in the front door. She poured a couple glasses of Sauvignon Blanc and handed him one as he entered the kitchen.

"Hi sweetheart," she said as he lowered his lips to hers. "Dinner is ready. Hate to rush it, but we have to be at the gallery early this evening."

"I really have a terrible headache honey. Would you understand if I didn't go with you? I hate missing your opening, but..."

Kate interrupted and said, "Alec, Stop. Of course you must stay home. You've not been yourself for a while. I'm worried. Will you please see Dr. Wilson soon?"

"You're right Kate; I've been feeling rather punk lately. Too many headaches; I'll call for an appointment next week."

After dinner, Kate retreated to their bedroom to dress for the evening opening of her latest photographs; Alec sat in his big chair in the study, with Bailey at his side, and watched the evening news. As Kate grabbed her coat from the closet, he came out and gave her a hug and said, "Sorry sweetie I can't be with you. Drive carefully and I will see you later this evening."

"I love you," she said and quickly dashed to the car.

Chapter Four

Now approaching their old rock house high on the hill overlooking town, Kate once again relived the moment she had stepped out of the steamy shower, and the realization of how she might lose the love of her life overcame her and the tears began to flow. And now as then, she searched for clarity. Somehow the answers would be found.

Bailey came over to Kate as she stepped out of her car. She gave him a big hug and said, "Daddy is getting better and will be home soon". But he seemed uneasy and kept stepping in front of her as if to block her attempt to reach the front door. With the hair on his back raised, Bailey looked at her and then would look over to the house with a snarl, baring his white teeth. She knew the police had not started their surveillance yet, so she decided to call Bryan. Reaching into her bag to retrieve her phone she dialed his number. "Yea, this is Chief Harris," she heard on the other end.

"Bryan, Kate here, I just got home and by the way Bailey is acting, I have a strong suspicion someone might be inside the house again."

"Kate, get back in your car immediately and drive to the road. I'll be there in a few minutes."

As she turned and walked towards the car, an arm grabbed her around the shoulder and neck; a coarse voice said, "Shut up and listen and I won't hurt you." He continued, "If you and your husband don't stop putting your nose where it doesn't belong, you'll be sorry."

Kate attempted to squirm and kick out of his strangle hold, but his grip held her tight. Her heart raced in fear. Bailey, with surprising strength and agility, and a terrifying growl, jumped on the man and within an instant his teeth ripped through cloth into flesh causing the man's arm to relax some around Kate's neck; he yelled in pain and struggled to free his blood soaked arm from Bailey's mouth; finally he pulled free, turned and ran through a grove of trees into the deep woods back of the house. Bailey started after him, but finally came back at Kate's insistence. Kate stood dazed. "Bailey", she said, looking at her normally friendly dog in wonder, "Good boy."

A minute later she heard the sound of an approaching siren. Bryan hopped out of the police car and Kate quickly told him what happened while he called for backup. When the canine police team arrived they began their search of the grounds and Bryan and Kate went into the house to find it had been searched again; this time the burglar had located the safe but found it empty.

The policemen and dog came back with the handcuffed bloodied man who had attacked Kate. They loaded him in the caged area of the police car and when the Chief and patrol car left, Kate and Bailey walked back into the house and with the fear in her heart passing, she sat on the large sectional with Bailey across her lap and closed her eyes, hoping for a moments escape from the nightmare that seemed to surround her.

Later that evening, after a hot shower and quick dinner, Kate again left for the hospital. As Kate entered Alec's room, she saw him awake, his eyes turning to greet her. With a burst of joy, she went to his side and put her head against his chest, "Oh my darling, thank God. How long have you been awake?"

"I just now looked around trying to figure out where I am and why I'm here and there you were," He said with a puzzled look on his drawn, but handsome face. Alec put his arm around her and held her close. Speaking through her tears, Kate said, "It's been two weeks Alec. When I got home after my opening I found you all but unconscious on the bed and you told me you had already called the paramedics. They soon rushed you to the hospital and you've been unconscious ever since." She softly kissed his pale lips and asked, "You haven't seen anyone; nurses, Dr. Wilson, your parents?"

"No, as I said, I just woke up and tried to grasp the meaning of everything. I don't remember anything since you left for the gallery and I felt sick and went to the bedroom to lie down."

Kate rang for the nurse who went to call the doctor and her heart felt overjoyed with the fear of the past weeks melting away. When Paul arrived, he told Alec about his condition and prognosis. Later that evening, when Alec seemed stronger, Kate told him about her meeting with Bryan, and hoped he would understand why she had to turn over the CD's to the Chief. Alec listened without a word, seemingly able to follow the details. When Alec fell asleep, Kate pushed back his tousled hair, kissed him on his forehead and told him she loved him very much and would see him first thing in the morning.

The next day, when Alec seemed stronger and more alert, Bryan came by and together they told him about the break-in and the prints found in the study belonged to two men working for the oil company, and another to the reporter Alec had hired. Along with these men, two corporate executive and the site engineer would also be charged. Bryan felt that these indictments should awaken other companies in the valley to clean up and secure their storage facilities and also be required to use anti-pollution devices to help restore the damage they had done. He also confirmed finding arsenic in the water container of the coffee maker at Alec's office. They decided to tell him about the attack on Kate when he was stronger.

Later that evening Kate sat next to Alec in the Garden Room of the hospital and squeezed his hand. She knew they soon would return to their home high on the bluff, overlooking the valley with the hazy blue mountains to the west. What new adventures, she wondered, would they face together in the future.

ANOTHER POINT OF VIEW

"Call me Moby Dick," the very large white whale said to Amanda, a smaller sperm whale munching on a mouthful of tasty squid. "I have traveled far and wide across endless waters to find a peaceful place to settle down and start a family. Before I can find my bliss, I am chased by strange looking creatures, in wooden floaters with expansive white leaves that catch the wind. When they see me, they run and jump into smaller floaters and chase me with long, sharp sticks. I hear them call me a monster; yet it is they who terrorize me. Remote waters have become my home and my affliction. I wait to fight again and again."

Moby Dick was not born to fight; he had a peaceful heart. The first harpoon entering his side caused a searing pain which caused him to dive and pull the harpoon thrower down with him; he then came up underneath and with his large nose pushed the boat high into the sky. With each fight his reputation grew and more sailors in their ships came looking for him.

Ahab was a whale hunter who had earlier lost his leg in a battle with Moby Dick. The large white whale caught him with his sickle-shaped lower jaw and "reaped away Ahab's leg, as a mower a blade of grass in the field." From that time onward, Ahab's obsession was to kill Moby Dick; at any cost to himself or crew. After many months, days and hours searching the Pacific waters, Ahab and his crew came upon Moby Dick near sunset. The crew wanted to wait until morning to hunt Moby, but Ahab, who had been driven crazy with his obsession of killing the white whale, insisted on starting immediately. As the harpoon sailors left in their small boat, Moby

Dick laid low in the water. When the mother ship had brought down its sails and was motionless in the water, Moby Dick raised his large head and with all his power he smashed into the ship. The water poured into the large hole drowning all the screaming sailors.

Ahab, still out in the small harpoon boat, did not know he had lost his ship. When Moby Dick appeared in his site, he stood on his peg leg holding his harpoon yelling, "Ho, ho! We have you now monster." Moby Dick felt pain in his side and flew forward; the line attached to the harpoon went flying and wrapped around Ahab's neck. Moby Dick dove deep pulling the screaming, crazed Ahab to the depths. The rest of the crew searching the late evening horizon found only debris in the water and realized the ship had been lost. Suddenly, large concentric circles of frothy waves surrounded them; the large white whale closed the ring and their fate.

About the Author

Leigh Clarke studied creative writing at the on-line Writer's University, completing a one year MFA program, a class on writing the short story, another on completing a novel, and several others that enriched her knowledge of creative writing.

She received her BFA in Studio Art in 1997, from the Art Institute of San Miguel, sponsored by the University of Guanajuato, Mexico. She also studied Mexican Art History and Greek and Roman Art and Literature.

Born in the western state of Wyoming in the 30's, her point of view was influenced by the visual and written history of the West that surrounded her; where the Sioux roamed and established their winter camps, and western ranchers, like her father, and grandfathers before him, attempted to survive the Great Depression, a major draught, and a World War. These events shaped her early years and taught that hardship and discipline meant survival for a nation and its people.

She raised her three children mostly as a single parent and has lived a long life of good health and love for family; including her three grandchildren. She presently lives in the North Texas Hill Country with her two pups, Beau and Bandit.

Ms. Clarke has published a book, *A Land Above*, a story about the first generation of her family arriving in Charleston, South Carolina from Northern Ireland in 1797, is working on Part II of this story, *A New Land,* and also has a memoir in final draft.